Julia McNair Wright

Twelve Noble Men

Julia McNair Wright

Twelve Noble Men

ISBN/EAN: 9783337780210

Printed in Europe, USA, Canada, Australia, Japan

Cover: Foto ©Andreas Hilbeck / pixelio.de

More available books at **www.hansebooks.com**

TWELVE NOBLE MEN.

BY

Mrs. JULIA McNAIR WRIGHT.

PHILADELPHIA:

PRESBYTERIAN BOARD OF PUBLICATION,

No. 1334 CHESTNUT STREET.

CONTENTS.

4 *CONTENTS.*

I.

ONE OF GOD'S SPARROWS:

THE STORY OF MARTIN BOOZ.

Twelve Noble Men.

I.

ONE OF GOD'S SPARROWS:

THE STORY OF MARTIN BOOZ.

ONCE, when Jesus was preaching, he said to the people, to encourage them to trust in God's care for them, "Are not five sparrows sold for two farthings? and not one of them is forgotten before God. Fear not, therefore, ye are of more value than many sparrows."

I have a story to tell you of one who all his life was like a poor lonely, helpless sparrow, but God took care of him, and also made him a great blessing. This man was of more value than millions of sparrows, but he often learned a lesson from the wee chirping birds. His name was MARTIN BOOZ, and he was born in Bavaria about a hundred years ago. When I tell you that Martin had fifteen brothers and sisters, you will say, "Oh, here is a whole family of little sparrows at once!" And, sure enough, the house was like a full nest of noisy young birds. Mr. Booz was a farmer; he had a small red house, green fields, green hedges, a barn, twenty cows and four horses. There were two children younger than Martin, and the eldest of all the family was a girl named Kate. She was eighteen, and a good sister. When Martin was five years old a terrible disease broke out in his neighborhood. First the babies of his family—two small boys—died; then Martin's mother; then two of his little sisters; then his father. Twelve orphan children were now left in the home of Mr. Booz; they were God's sparrows, and he cared for them. The farm, the cows and the horses were sold, and the money was used in getting the boys and girls into good homes and schools. The eldest sister was going to be married, and all were provided for but little Martin. What should be done with him? Kate had a good thought. Her mother had a brother living in the city of Augsburg. He was a rich lawyer, and his name was Koegel. He had never seemed to care for his sister or her children. Kate said she meant to take Martin to him; she was sure he would love such a cunning little fellow. One Monday morning, early in autumn, Kate rose up long before day, washed and dressed her little brother, making him look his best, then put some lunch of bread and cheese in her pocket, and set out to walk to Augsburg.

Martin was a stout, hearty child, but he was very young, and of course he soon grew tired. When he was tired Kate took him on her back and trudged on. It was a long way to go, and by afternoon Martin was weary, cross and sleepy, and poor Kate felt as if she could hardly carry him any longer. She turned into a cornfield and sat down. She looked at Martin's red, cross face and said, "My lad, your uncle Koegel won't like your looks if he sees you in this state." She then made a bed of cornstalks, laid Martin in it, sat by him until he fell asleep, and then, covering him with her shawl, prepared to walk the remaining two miles into Augsburg and see her uncle. She asked God to take care of her little brother when she left him thus alone.

Poor Martin ! was he not now like a little lost bird, left alone in the cornfield ? Kate went to her uncle and told him all the family trouble. She explained how the twelve children had all been provided for except little Martin, and that she wanted Uncle Koegel to adopt him.

"Very well," said her uncle. "There is no denying he is my sister's son, and I suppose I must take him, but I and my wife know little about children. I do not see what they are good for."

"To make men and women," said Kate.

"You may bring me the child. I cannot go to fetch him; my time is worth money," said Counselor Koegel.

"He will be here in two hours," said Kate.

"Where, then, have you left him ?" asked he.

"Asleep in a cornfield," replied the sister.

Kate's heart was light, and she walked briskly to get her little brother. She knew that though her uncle was queer and cold he would not be unkind, but had means to provide for Martin.

The boy was pleasanter after his long nap. Kate washed his rosy cheeks, curled his yellow hair, gave him a pretzel which she had bought in the city, and, taking him by the hand, soon led him into the presence of their uncle.

"How did you fetch him?" asked Mr. Koegel.

"On my back from home," said the sturdy Kate.

"Thou art a brave girl," said he, smiling. "Stay a few days and I will give you a present."

"Yes, stay," said his wife, "or the boy will be lonely. I cannot abide the crying of a child."

Martin did not fancy staying at Augsburg. He cried to go back with his sister to his former home. Finding he could not be consoled, Kate rose early on the third day, and, leaving Martin asleep, set out for her old abode.

When Martin found her gone he screamed and sobbed.

"What is to be done with him?" asked his aunt at breakfast when he could not eat for crying.

"He is too old for a nurse," said his uncle, uneasily.

"Let us send him to school; he will then be out of the way," said the aunt.

"Very good," said his uncle. So, after breakfast, he took the child to an old school-master who taught children from eight in the morning until five at evening, giving them recess and an hour at noon to go home for dinner. Here Martin stayed year after year. His uncle and aunt provided him food and clothes and took him to church on Sundays, but never taught him anything, never even asked what he learned or how he got on: they scarcely knew if he had learned to read.

One day, when Martin was eleven years old, he went to his uncle early in the morning, saying, "Please sir, it is quarter-day. Will you give me money to pay for my schooling?"

His uncle cried out roughly, "There it is! school-money again! Why, I've sent you to school this six years, and it is quite time I put you to learn a trade, where you could make your living. Pray, boy, what would you like to be?"

Martin hung his head and said bashfully, "If you please, uncle, I would like to go to school and learn enough to be a clergyman. I do not like a trade."

"You a clergyman!" cried his uncle loudly. "Why, you have neither money nor brains enough for that."

Here was a sad rebuff for poor Martin. He went and sat on a stone bench behind the back door and cried bitterly.

Pretty soon he heard his uncle calling: "Come, sir, come eat your breakfast, and then take a note from me to your schoolmaster. I'll know the merits of your case soon."

The note was to ask the master what sort of a boy Martin was in school. The answer was to be sent when Martin returned to dinner. The old schoolmaster had ever been Martin's best friend; he wrote very kindly to Mr. Koegel. He said that Martin was the best and smartest boy in school, that he was a very good Latin scholar, and that it would be a great sin to cut short the studies of a lad of such promise.

Now, while Martin is taking home this note, let us see how God had thus far cared for his little sparrow.

"When thy father and thy mother forsake thee, then the Lord will take thee up," says Scripture. When Martin's father and mother had died God had raised up protectors for him: God had given him food, clothes and shelter for his body. God had also given him the schoolmaster as a friend to cheer his little lonely heart; and now, when Martin's mind was like a flower opening into beautiful blossom, we will see how God provided for that.

When Mr. Koegel read the note he smiled; he was so pleased to hear that Martin was a smart boy that he whistled half a tune; then he said, "Latin, ho! ho! ho! Latin, lad;

why did thee not tell me of this Latin sooner ?"

"I was afraid you would think me looking too high for a poor boy if I mentioned Latin."

"Latin !" said Koegel, reading the note again. "'Oh, and a smart boy is he, and a good boy.' Come now, lad, shake hands; you shall go to college and be a clergyman."

Martin's family were Roman Catholics. His uncle did not ask him if it was because he loved God, and desired to serve him and help men to be better, that he chose to be a clergyman. No ; he knew Martin only wished to be this that he might have a good house, money to live on and plenty of study. Martin and his uncle and his schoolmaster all thought these views right ; they knew of no other. Mr. Koegel sent Martin to the college of the Jesuits of St. Salvador. He studied there five years. He was now nearly a young man, and was called a good scholar. He was about to study logic at the lyceum, and as it was vacation he went home to his uncle.

The moment Mr. Koegel met Martin after his absence he cried, " Where have you been all this while? I hope you are by this time a good scholar. Look you, Martin : I do not care about those Jesuits ; they do not make wise men of their pupils. To-morrow you are to start for the university at Dillingen ; so go back to-day to St. Salvador and get your diploma from those Jesuits, that the teachers at Dillingen may gladly receive you."

Martin got a horse and rode back to college to ask for his certificates of scholarship and good conduct, but the Jesuits would not give them to him. At Dillingen were some good, pious men among the teachers—one was named Sailer and another Zimmer—and many of their pupils were beginning to read their Bibles and think for themselves. The Jesuits hated this school. They were like men setting a trap to catch the soul of this poor sparrow. They said to him, " See here, Martin : Dillingen is a vile hole ; you will get no good there. Stay here with us, and we will get you a place as private tutor, where you will be well paid and you can study free of expense and have money in your pocket. Go tell your uncle that."

The Jesuits were very cunning; they knew Uncle Koegel was fond of money. But you know God says in his word that when his birds are caught in snares the snares shall be broken and the captives shall escape; and so it was in this case. The college of St. Salvador was on the edge of Augsburg, and Martin hurried back to his uncle to tell him what had been said by his teachers.

Mr. Koegel was not won by the hint of his nephew earning money. He flew into a passion, crying, " That is just like the Jesuits ! They hate all teachers but themselves. You are going to Dillingen ; and now go to the Jesuits and tell them if they don't give you your certificates I will find a way to make them."

The teachers were afraid of Counselor Koegel, and gave Martin his papers.

Martin went to Dillingen, a town in Bavaria, thinking, from what he had heard, that it would be a very bad place ; but he learned to love his good professors there, and was very happy. His teachers were so pleased with his

2

good conduct, polite, gentle manners and studious habits that they wrote to Mr. Koegel praising Martin highly. Mr. Koegel became kinder to his nephew when every one spoke well of him.

For four years Martin studied at Dillingen; he was now twenty years of age, had concluded his preparatory studies, and was ready to be made a priest. Martin had always been called a good lad. He had no knowledge of Jesus as a Saviour nor of himself as a great sinner; he thought himself a right good fellow, quite fit to be a priest, and, like the young man in the Bible, would have said, " What lack I yet?" His uncle thought of him in the same way.

Mr. Koegel was very anxious to have his nephew ordained a priest. Martin had been ill of a fever, and was afraid of failing in his examination, but he went to Augsburg with other young men, and passed with such credit that every one spoke well of him, and his own joy and pride were great. He was now made a priest, and was allowed to celebrate mass in a grand old church at Augsburg. His uncle was there, and more than five hundred people and thirty priests, who came to please the old counselor. Mr. Koegel was so proud and happy on account of his nephew's success that he did what we would call a very odd thing. He gave a party which lasted three days! Martin went to it, and liked it very greatly.

Martin studied some little while longer, and then got a place as preacher in a large town. The name of the town is so long that I would not like to bother little folks with it. The good teaching Martin Booz had had at Dillingen had made him willing to think. He was no idle trifler, and when he found himself preaching to poor ignorant souls every Sabbath, he began to wonder what he should say and do to make them live well and die happy.

I have shown you how God had cared for Martin's body and for his mind, and now I will tell you how he cared for his soul.

When Martin began to think about the state of his people he concluded that the best he could do would be to become a very holy man and live a most pious life before them. He did not know that only God can make a man holy, and that a holy life begins in a new heart—a heart washed in the blood of the Lord Jesus.

Martin Booz thought that the way to be holy was to fast often, to pray often, to give much to the poor, and to do whatever things were most disagreeable to himself. He was trying to find out his own way to heaven.

Martin was so earnest in his efforts to be very holy that people became interested in him, and, as they none of them knew more about true religion than he did, they believed he was a wonderful saint. He stayed in the church and burying-ground a great deal, and gave his own food to the poor. He was not pretending; he was really trying to be good. For this kind of goodness he was made head of a convent of Jesuits. This was a high honor, but it did not make him happy. He was called a holy man, but, as he said afterward, his goodness was all a form; he was afraid to die; he was full of care and sorrow; his soul had no rest; he was always crying, "What shall I do?"

Martin was so much liked by everybody who lived in the town that his brother-monks in the convent got jealous of him. They were not good men, and they hated him very much. They read his letters, tore his books, interrupted his prayers, called him ill names and talked unkindly of him. He was very wretched, and finally a good bishop who was his friend asked him if he would like to go to a little country church and be its priest.

"Oh yes, yes," said Martin eagerly.

"It would not be half so honorable as the place you have in the convent," said his friend.

"I do not mind that," said Martin, "if I may only have peace. My heart will break if I quarrel."

So Martin Booz went to the little poor church and began to teach the people as well as he could, but as yet he knew very little that was of real value. He was what the Bible calls "a blind leader of the blind." He was very good to the sick and poor, often visiting them. The Bible says, "He that waters shall be watered also himself," and you will now see how this was true in Martin's case.

One day he went to see a poor sick woman who was about to die; he tried to cheer her,

and said, " You will die very well and happily."

" Why so?" asked the poor dying woman
calmly.

" Because you have lived so well," replied
Booz. " Every one calls you a very good
woman, and says you have led a pious and
holy life. Of course you will die well."

The sick woman smiled, and then said
earnestly, " Mr. Booz, if I go out of this
world trusting to my own merits to save
me, I shall be lost. But I have a Saviour;
Jesus died for me, and so I can die happy.
Oh, sir, a clergyman like you ought to be
able to tell the dying about Christ and his
blood, which washes away sin. If I only
knew what you can tell me, how miserable
I would be! How could I stand before
God and answer for all my idle words?
How could I find in my life one truly good
and holy act? If Christ had not died for
me, I would be lost, sir. If I have lived a
Christian life, I have only lived it by his
grace. Jesus is my hope; he saves me; he
will make me happy in heaven; in him I
am happy now as I am dying."

Martin had come to this house to teach and to comfort; he found himself taught by this woman, who had learned the truth of God. Booz was not proud; he did not scorn the poor sick woman's words. On the contrary, he believed them. He said, "Here is what I have looked for; here is true faith. I will seek for Jesus as my Saviour; where shall I find him?" He asked this of the poor woman.

"You will find him in his book, the Bible," said she.

God says he will not suffer a proud heart, but he loves to dwell with a lowly spirit. Martin meekly took the poor dying woman for his teacher, and, as she had told him to study the Bible, he sought for one as soon as he got home. Now he was truly happy. He did not now carry the burden of his sins; he had laid them all on the dear Saviour. Now he could point men to the way of life; he no more bade them save themselves by fasts and alms, but he told them of the Lamb of God, who had paid all their debt. This was such new teaching in Austria, where Martin labored, that people flocked from all sides to hear it. In our country this good news is preached by thousands of ministers every week, but in Austria, especially in Martin's time, people dared not tell of salvation by Christ alone. As soon as Booz began to preach in this way the priests hated him, and did all they could against him. They did not dare to kill him, as they did holy men long ago, which I told you of in the lives of Huss and Wishart; but they drove Martin out of his home, took away his church and put him in prison.

I will tell you one little story to show how kind Martin was, and how God took care of him. Before Martin was driven from his home he buried a man and a woman who left an only child, a poor orphan boy. This boy stood crying by his parents' grave. Booz took him in his arms and comforted him, gave him the only shilling he had in the world, and led him to a house where some kind people let the forlorn child stay; and every day after that Booz took the boy and taught him to read and to serve God. By and by the boy was taken away by his relatives. He grew up to be a rich man, and was a colonel in the Austrian army. This was when Booz was old, poor and a prisoner. The officer found Booz in great misery, and though he could not take him out of prison, he visited him every day and brought everything he could find to make him more comfortable. If Booz said his friend was doing too much for him, the colonel would reply, "Oh no; you gave me your last shilling when I was a poor orphan boy; you loved me and taught me; and I like nothing better than to help you." This is what the Bible means when it says, "Cast thy bread on the waters, and thou shalt find it after many days."

Booz was in several prisons. He was sitting in one by the little window of his cell one day; he was lonely and hungry; he wanted to write and to read, but his cruel foes would not give him books, paper or pens. As he sat there he saw a string drop down before his window. After a while he took hold of it. Then some one from the roof above dropped him a roasted turkey tied to the string. Inside the turkey he found letters, a Testament, paper, a pen and a little bottle of ink. Don't you think that was very queer stuffing for a turkey?

He wrote letters to his friends, but did not know how to send them. His jailers would take them away if they knew of them. Each day some one walked in the hall by his cell and softly sang a line of Luther's hymn, " A strong tower is our God." Martin knew that was a friend looking for letters. He looked on the floor and saw a little mouse running out by a hole he had gnawed under the door. " Very good," said Booz; and, rolling his letter up small, he pushed it out after the mouse, and the singing friend got it. Soon there was an answer sent the same way. How odd! This was the mouse-hole post-office, wasn't it?

Thus you see how God cared for Martin's soul, and sent him knowledge of Jesus by the mouth of the poor woman; and when Martin got put in prison for Christ's sake, God cared for him still, and sent him friends and help one way and another.

After a long while and after many troubles Booz was let out of prison and got a little church at Sayn. The night he left prison some friends met in a house to welcome him. He went there, but was so pale and thin that they did not recognize him until he said, "What! don't you know me?" Then how they crowded about him!

Martin Booz did much good work at Sayn. He was getting old and feeble, and as he lived alone some of his distant friends said, "What will become of him? He may be ill and die all alone." "Oh," said Martin, "I am God's sparrow, and he will take care of me, just as he always has done."

Sure enough, it was so. One day Martin sat in an arbor by himself. He was very weak, and felt sad. A young man with a traveling-bag in his hand entered the gate. He had come a long way; he had heard of good Martin Booz, and God had put it in his heart to come and live with him and take care of him.

The young man said to Martin, "I will be your son; I will help you teach your people. I will nurse you when you are sick, and I will read to you when you are blind."

Did not God take good care of Martin Booz?

The young man stayed there as long as Booz lived. Martin died very happily; he had no fear and no pain. His last words were, "Lord, into thy hands I commend my spirit." Then he went home to heaven. Is it not a happy lot to be one of God's sparrows?

II.

THE INNKEEPER'S SON:

THE STORY OF GEORGE WHITEFIELD.

II.

THE INNKEEPER'S SON:

THE STORY OF GEORGE WHITEFIELD.

ALMOST every boy thinks he would like to be famous, even those boys who are too lazy to do anything to earn fame. Fame does not grow out of the ground without trouble, like a thistle or a mullein-stalk; it is rather like wheat or peaches, which must be carefully cultivated and toiled for. One boy says he would like to be famous as a soldier; another thinks he would like to be famous for wit; another for learning; another for riches and grand style of living; but the best of all is to be famous for doing good.

I shall tell you now of a boy who became very famous as a preacher. He did a great deal of good. He did not do good because he wanted to make a name by it, but because he loved God and desired to serve him. This boy's name was GEORGE. His father's name was Whitefield, and he kept a tavern. George had five brothers, all older than himself.

His troubles and the troubles of his family seemed to begin as soon as George was born. While he was a small baby his mother was very ill for some months. As she lay in her bed, with little George in his cradle at her side, she would look at him for hours and pray for him a great deal. It seemed to be in her mind even then that this child would grow up to be a great comfort to her. She was a pious woman, and hoped her son would give his heart early to God.

When George was but two years old his father died. Mrs. Whitefield, after her husband's death, kept the tavern herself and tried to make a living for her six sons. She had hard work. She was very busy all day, and to get George out of her way and out of mischief she sent him early to a dame's school. George was a lively little lad, and he hated to go to school and study; he had rather be out of doors hunting birds' nests and making dams in the gutters. Very likely, the dame did not understand teaching very well. One day a good minister stopped at Mrs. Whitefield's house. Some children were playing in the yard with George. They were Scotch and Irish, and the minister asked them several questions; by and by he asked George where he was born.

"In an inn," said George smartly.

"So was the dear Lord Jesus," said the stranger.

This impressed George very much. The minister was so kind that the boy after tea went to talk with him, and heard the whole story of Jesus, who was born in the stable of an inn and laid in a manger.

After this George always showed a great love for ministers, and if any of them were in the house he liked to stand near them and listen to their talk. He also loved to go to church, and instead of sleeping or playing during the sermon he listened with all his might.

One Sunday evening, when George and

3

his mother were sitting quietly together, she
told him how she had prayed for him, and
that she expected him to be a great help
and comfort to her, even more than any of
his brothers.

George loved his mother, and he never
forgot these words. If he was tempted to
do anything very wicked he would say to
himself, " I must not ; this is no way to grow
up to be my mother's comfort."

Still, during these days, though there were
some very nice things about George, he was
not a Christian boy. He had not true love
for God in his heart, and often did things
which he knew to be wrong and neglected
things which he ought to do. George was
wasteful of his money, idle about his studies,
fond of tricks which troubled other people,
and would read books which he should not
have looked into. Thus he grew up in the
noble old city of Gloucester, at the Bell Inn,
until he was ten years old. At this time Mrs.
Whitefield married again, and, unfortunately,
she married a bad man, who made trouble in
her family, neglected her business and wasted
her money. She still managed to keep George

at school, but several of his brothers, having grown up, left home to learn trades and take care of themselves. At school George loved to learn pieces to speak, and as he did it well his masters were pleased to hear him. He was not now at the dame's school, but at the grammar school of St. Mary de Crypt. This was quite a famous place, and often visited by the city magistrates and people from a distance, and George was often called on to make speeches to them. He did this so well and gracefully that they often made him presents of money. Too much pocket-money is a temptation to boys, and George fell in with bad company which did him much harm. He stopped at this school until he was sixteen.

At this time all his brothers were gone from home, his step-father was idle and his poor mother's business was in a very bad state; her inn was badly kept, and she could hardly pay her debts and get any clothes. George pitied his mother and longed to help her. He told her he knew quite enough to leave school and get a place where he could earn money. He tried very hard to do this, but could find no work. He then determined to remain at home and help his mother in the inn. She felt very sad at this, for she wanted George to be a fine scholar. However, there seemed no help for it, so George got a leathern apron, hung a pair of snuffers for trimming candles at his belt, and became in all things like the hired boy they call a *drawer* in English taverns. He washed mops, scrubbed floors and windows, cleaned candlesticks, served out beer, waited at table, ran errands and watered horses. This he did for a year and a half. During this time he read everything he could get hold of; when ministers were at the house he hung about the room where they sat; he went to preaching as often as he could, and began to amuse himself by writing sermons. One of these, which he thought very fine, he presented to his oldest brother, who was married and living in Bristol. He liked to read prayers from the prayer-book as the ministers did, trying to see how well he could make them sound, and he was now very sorry that he had not made a better use of his time in school.

He at this time found a friend in a very pious youth, who urged him to study his Bible and to go to Oxford College to learn to be a minister. George would always say, "I wish I could." His mother often heard this talk as her son was doing his work in the tavern, and she wished with all her heart that her boy could go to Oxford. But how could he go without money?

He began to read the Bible at his friend's request, and liked it so much that he studied it when he was sitting up at night waiting for guests or for men to finish their drinking and leave the tap-room.

His mother's difficulties became so great, in spite of George's help, that she sold out her business to one of her grown-up sons and took part of a little house for herself. George stopped with his brother as drawer for a few weeks, but they did not get on well together, so he went to his oldest brother at Bristol to look for work. Work was scarce, and in a month George went back to his mother. In all this time God was leading George, but he did not know it. One day, while George was thus living without work at his mother's and wondering what he should do, a young man who had sometimes lodged at the Bell Inn came to call on her. This young man was what is called a *servitor* in Oxford at the college. He worked for his board and his tuition, and managed to earn enough from the rich students to buy his clothes.

"How do you come on?" asked George's mother.

"Pretty well," said the young man. "I get my education, and that is something to be thankful for."

"Indeed it is," said she; "I wish my George could do the same."

"This last term, when I got through," he said, "I paid all I owed, and had clothes for vacation on hand. I had just one penny remaining in my purse."

"Why, this will do for my son," cried the mother; and turning to George, who stood by, she said, "My son, will you go to Oxford as a servitor and be educated?"

"With all my heart, mother," said George eagerly.

George at once went back to the grammar

school, and studied so well that when he was eighteen he went to college and became a servitor.

He found many of the students so wicked that he was afraid of them, and for the most part of his time he shut himself in his room and worked at his books as hard as he could. But at this college were some young men different from all the rest; they led pious lives and said their chief desire was to serve God. The leaders of this party were two brothers named Wesley, about whom I shall write my next story. How much George longed to know these young men! But he was very poor, and they were pretty rich, and he thought that they would be ashamed of his company. He did not know that truly pious people have none of these silly notions, but feel that all who love the dear Saviour become brothers in him. The Bible says, "The rich and poor meet together, and the Lord is the Maker of them all." This is to teach us not to be proud and scornful. The Bible also says, "All ye are brethren." Brothers, you know, ought to love and help each other.

A whole year went by, during which George watched the Wesleys afar off. At length one day he went to visit a poor woman who was in great sorrow—so great that she had even tried to kill herself. George advised her to send for Mr. Charles Wesley to pray with her.

Wesley had often noticed George walking by himself, and he made up his mind to get acquainted with him. He wrote George a note saying that he had called on the poor woman, and asking George to come the next morning and take breakfast with him. After that they were dear friends.

George was now anxious to serve God and deeply sorry for all his sins, but he did not see how ready Jesus is to forgive us and wash away our guilt. His trouble of mind made him sick, and he lay in bed burning with fever. No one was with him, and he wanted a drink very much, and could not get it. This made him think of the good Jesus on the cross when he said, "I thirst." His mind turned to the sufferings and death of Christ. "If he died for me," said George, "he is surely quite willing to save me. Why may I not now trust my soul to him and be happy at once?" He felt that he might. He cried out that dear little prayer, "Lord, I believe; help thou my unbelief!" How happy was George now that he had found a Saviour indeed! It almost made him well of his fever. George now loved nothing so much as to tell people of Jesus. He spent his time when he was not studying in visiting poor people, prisons and hospitals. Some of his friends wanted him to begin to preach at once, but he said, "No, I mean to have a hundred and fifty sermons ready first." This was trusting to his sermons more than to God, and you shall see how the Lord taught him better than that.

He was not very well, and he went home to see his mother. A clergyman came to urge him to preach, but George said, "Oh no; I cannot do well enough; I am too ignorant. I will lend you a sermon to show you how badly I write and preach yet."

The minister took the sermon, and in two weeks came back saying, "This is a very good sermon. I preached it to my people, and they liked it very much. There are five dollars for my use of it."

That was a queer way to do. Ministers write their own sermons now-a-days.

George wrote and talked so much about religion that people said he was crazy. Wicked people often call those crazy who love God. They did so hundreds of years ago, when Paul was living and preaching.

When George was twenty-one years old he was so well known for wisdom and piety that his friends begged him to delay no longer, but to begin preaching at once. Whitefield prayed to God, saying, like Moses when God called to him from the bush, "Lord, I cannot go; I am too weak, too young; no one will hear me. I shall be proud and foolish, and do more harm than good." But God was able to preserve his soul. Still Whitefield prayed, "Lord, do not send me yet." But the words came into his mind, "Nothing shall pluck you out of my hands." Then he felt that God was able and willing to help him, and he consented to be ordained. He says that when he went up to be ordained before all the people in the great church he could only think of the little boy Samuel standing in the tabernacle wearing his linen ephod, and in his heart he prayed God to help him to live only for his glory and the good of souls.

When he preached his first sermon he spoke with so much fervor and power that people wept, and some bad men went to the bishop, saying, "This fellow Whitefield has driven fifteen folks mad with his first sermon."

"I hope," said the bishop, "that these fifteen will not get over what you call their 'madness' before next Sunday."

This Bishop Benson was a very good man; he was Whitefield's true friend, and often helped him.

From the very beginning of his ministry George Whitefield was a great preacher. God had given him grand gifts to use in his service. He had a wonderful voice, a beautiful face, a warm heart, a great love of souls and plenty of earnest words to tell of Jesus and his grace. People said he was like the angel John tells us of in Revelation, flying between heaven and earth bearing the everlasting gospel to preach to men. All Whitefield cared for was to serve God; in this work he never seemed to grow tired, to think of himself or to have any vanity. He used to say, "Let my name and memory perish; I do not care for that. All I want is to have God glorified and sinners saved."

When a proud man said to him, "Do you believe we shall see that Methodist Wesley in heaven?" George replied very meekly, "No; I suppose he will be so much higher and nearer God than we are that he will be clear out of our sight." You see, he was meek, and Christ says, "Blessed are the meek."

George Whitefield was indeed blessed—in his life, his work, his contented heart and his happy death. From the first of his preaching Whitefield met with very wonderful success. Crowds came to listen to him until no building could hold them. As he was anxious to do all the good possible, he began to speak in the open air. He would choose some balcony, high platform or window, and speak from that; and his voice was

so strong that he could make thousands
hear him. Before long he was invited to
visit America; John Wesley wrote for him
to come and preach in Georgia. He wrote:
" Do you ask me what you shall have? Food
to eat, raiment to put on, a house to lay your
head in—such as our Lord had not—and a
crown of glory which fadeth not away."
Some people would not have been satisfied
without the promise of money and honor,
but George Whitefield says his " heart
leaped up in him " to get so grand a chance
of doing good. He first came to our country in 1737. His first home was at Savan-
nah, Georgia. On the voyage here he did
all he could to teach the people on board his
ship, and he did them much good. Finding
a newspaper one day on the captain's pillow,
he laid in its place a little tract, which was
the means of this captain's becoming a pious
man. He was asked while on the ship to
marry a couple; while he was doing so the
young man began to laugh and act silly.
Whitefield stopped the marriage service and
talked to him so very solemnly about his
duty that presently the man and all those

near began to weep. The men on shipboard said Mr. Whitefield taught them nothing but good, and could make a text out of everything that happened.

Whitefield went from this country to England and back again a number of times. He was dearly loved everywhere, but in England there was a deal of fault found because he preached out of doors and in other places than churches. He was often called crazy and a fanatic, but he did not mind ridicule or unkindness; all he cared for was to please the Lord. He preached very often in Philadelphia; one of his favorite places for service was the balcony in front of the old courthouse. There is an old church in Freehold, New Jersey, where he loved to preach; it is called the Tennent Church. In Philadelphia, Mr. Whitefield preached sometimes to as many as fifteen thousand people at once. Can you imagine such a crowd as that? We are told that during a year that he stayed in Philadelphia there was preaching twice every day and three or four times on Sunday. Who can tell me how many sermons that would be in the year?

I cannot tell you all about a long life spent in doing good—in building churches, colleges and orphan asylums. Our country owes a great deal to George Whitefield, the son of the keeper of the Bell Inn, Gloucester.

I shall tell you two or three things which happened in his preaching, and then see if you do not think you would love to hear such a preacher.

One day he was preaching to some sailors. He talked to them about their lives as if life was a voyage; he said: " Well, my boys, we have a fine sky, we go swiftly over a smooth sea, and we shall soon lose sight of land. But what means this sudden darkness and that black cloud on the western sky? Hark! don't you hear the thunder? Look! don't you see the lightning? There is a storm coming. Every man to his place! How the big waves dash against our ship! The air is dark, the storm is high. Our masts are gone! What next?"

The sailors had got so interested that they seemed to see all this, and all together they leaped up and shouted out, " Take to the long-boats, sir!"

Once, when Mr. Whitefield was preaching in Boston, in the middle of the sermon a terrible thunderstorm arose. It grew very dark, the thunder pealed, the lightning blazed over all the sky. People were greatly terrified; some cried out, some sobbed, some fainted. Mr. Whitefield stepped to one side of the pulpit, stretched out his arms and repeated in a clear voice this beautiful hymn:

> "Hark! the Eternal rends the sky!
>   A mighty voice before him goes—
> A voice of music to his friends,
>   But threatening thunder to his foes:
> 'Come, children, to your Father's arms,
>   Hide in the shelter of my grace,
> Till the fierce storm be overblown,
>   And my revenging fury cease.'"

I hope my readers will learn this hymn. Mr. Whitefield had the people sing it, and by the time they finished the storm was over and all their hearts were impressed with a sense of God's great power and mercy.

At another time Mr. Whitefield was preaching out of doors at Baskingridge, New Jersey. Very many people wept on account of their sins; one little boy had his heart so touched that he cried aloud. Mr. Whitefield was standing in a wagon, and this child sat on the back seat. He lifted him up beside him, saying, "Friends, I will let this little seven-year-old boy preach for me. If such a child must cry and wail because he is a sinner, what must you do who have for years gone on in sin and despised the grace of God?" God blessed these words very greatly.

Once, in Wales, Mr. Whitefield was preaching at the edge of some woods. He was standing on a stump, and had a great crowd before him. Some bad people had come with stones and clubs, and threatened to kill him. They swore and called names. Mr. Whitefield was brave at first, but at last the men were so wild that he began to get a little afraid. His wife stood near him, and she pulled his coat. Did she tell him to run and hide? Oh no! Brave woman that she was, she said, "George, play the man for your God!" His courage returned, he spoke bravely, put the evil men to shame, and many people were converted.

Mr. Whitefield loved children; I think all good people do. They wrote him letters and liked to visit him, and he loved to teach them and pray for them.

4

Mr. Whitefield came to America seven times. He died in this country when he was fifty-six years old. He died quite suddenly, but he had lived near to God and was ready to go to him in heaven. He was buried in the Old South Church at Newburyport, Massachusetts. He died at the house of the pastor of this church, who was his dear friend. He had been a minister for thirty-four years, and who can count the souls saved by his means? Was not his a grand life to live? What is better than thus, like Jesus, to go about doing good? We can only do this when we have first gone to Jesus and got new hearts, washed in his blood and full of his love.

III.

THE TWO BROTHERS:

THE STORY OF JOHN AND CHARLES WESLEY.

III.

THE TWO BROTHERS:

THE STORY OF JOHN AND CHARLES WESLEY.

WHEN children read of great and good people, I think they like best to know what these people felt and did when they were children. In this story of two brothers my little friends will enjoy hearing where and how the brothers lived when they were small boys. JOHN and CHARLES were the youngest sons of Mr. Samuel Wesley, who was a minister in the village of Epworth in England. Mr. Wesley and his wife were very kind and pious people. They were quite poor, and there were so many children in the family that it was very hard to get food and clothes for them all. In those days people treated their ministers very meanly; they are not free from that fault now, but things are not so bad as they were. What will you think when I tell you that poor Mr. Wesley had to borrow money for fuel and to pay the doctor, and then was put in jail because he had not the money to pay back what he borrowed just when his creditor wanted it? The house where they lived was twice burned down, and each time Mr. Wesley had to build it at his own expense, though it belonged to the church, and not to him. If he had not rebuilt it he would have had no home, and then what would have become of all those little children?

The eldest son of the Wesleys was named Samuel, and he was a wise and good boy; he was sixteen years old when Charles was born, and John was then five. The house had already been once burned down, and it had cost so much to rebuild it that money was very scarce. The first wish of the parents was to have their children love God; the next object was to have them well educated. They said, " We are so poor we can never leave our children any money, but let us give them good educations, and they will always be able to take care of themselves. Wisdom is better than rubies."

Mrs. Wesley believed that people should begin to teach their children when they are little babies. I wish all mothers thought this; we should not then see so many naughty children. You say, "What can you teach a baby?" Why, you can teach it good habits; you can teach it to eat and sleep at a regular time, and not to scream after things. Mrs. Wesley never gave her children things that they cried after for the sake of keeping them still.

She loved her children, and tried to make them happy. Some of her rules were these: To teach her children to *cry softly.* What a pity all children do not learn that! Then we should have no roaring as if a leg was broken—all for what? Why, because some little body cannot get a gate open or has lost his ball. Another rule was that they must mind the first time they were spoken to. That is a good rule. Why not the first time as well as the sixth? To honor your parents is to *mind quickly and cheer-*

fully. Children who begin by obeying their parents will go on by obeying God. Mrs. Wesley also taught her children, even the very wee ones, to be quiet at prayer-time; also to know Sunday from other days, and keep it, in their baby fashion, as a day quieter and better than the rest. When her little children went to church they sat still, paid attention, and when they came home were able to tell something that they had heard.

Then these children were taught to eat what was given them at table, and not fret and quarrel with their food; they were not allowed to run about eating cake or pie between meals; therefore, when they came to the table they were ready to eat plain, good food. Having learned how to eat what was given them, they also knew how to take medicine without a fuss when it was needful; but these little boys and girls were not often ill. They were expected to be gentle and unselfish to each other, and to speak civilly to the servants.

By keeping these rules they were a happy family. For all there were so many of them, the sound of crying and quarreling was never heard in the house. People said that in all England there were no better brought-up children than Mrs. Wesley's. Their mother writes of them: "Never were children in better order; never were children better disposed to piety." Quarreling, lying or bad language was never heard among them.

The mother taught her girls entirely herself, and her boys until they were old enough to go off to a grammar school. After the alphabet-card the Bible was their first lesson book; in it they learned to read and spell. They were all bright children; the mother says that Samuel was the smartest, and Kezzy was the dullest. When set to learn a lesson they were not to leave it until it was perfect. In their little school-room at home, where their mother was the teacher, they kept the order they must have observed in a large school.

Once each week this good mother talked privately with each child about its soul and the way to get a new heart.

Thus in this home matters went on very pleasantly until John was six years old and

Charles was a small baby. Samuel was off at college. One night there was a cry of fire; the house was in flames; nothing could save it. So many little children were to be got out; how do you think they saved them all? Poor John was very nearly burned to death, but at last he was got out unhurt just before the floor of his room fell through. Dear me! what a time! And worst of all was, that their furniture and nearly all their clothes were gone, and now they had no house to go to; they were without a home. There was no help for it; they must scatter about as they could until the poor father built his house again. Where money is scarce it takes a long time to do anything. The father and mother and babies went to one place—the children here, there and everywhere. It was a whole year after this dreadful fire before the Wesley family were together again. Thirteen years after their mother, in a letter to her brother, said: " Mr. Wesley built his house in a year, but so poor are we that to this day it is not half furnished nor are any of us half well clad." Once, when a friend asked Mrs. Wesley if her fam-

A brand from the burning.　　　　　　　Page 58.

ily had ever been without food, she replied,
" No, I do not think that we were ever really
hungry, but we often found it such hard work
to get and pay for the plainest food that to
me it was about as hard as going without."

When the children were once more together their mother found great cause for grief.
While they had been scattered from their
parents they had been with improper company; had learned in many ways to neglect
the Sabbath; had run too much in the streets;
had read books and learned songs of a kind
which their mother did not approve; and
had begun to speak rudely and coarsely.
Now, very much of this careful mother's
work was to be done over again. Her heart
ached, but she kept her courage up. She
called her children about her and talked se-
riously with them of her troubles. She had
them help her make a set of laws for the rule
of the family, and these she wrote out plainly and hung up where all could see them.
Some of these laws were — that if a child
confessed a fault frankly it should not be
punished for it; if a child gave away anything he could not take it back; no one must

meddle with anything belonging to another without the consent of the owner; when any one did right, especially if it was in something hard for him, he was to be praised; if he did wrong while trying to do right, he must not be ridiculed or scolded, but must be gently taught how to do better; no child was to be scolded or punished twice for the same act.

Besides these excellent rules, Mrs. Wesley gave yet more time than formerly to religious teaching. She began and closed school each day by singing a psalm. Her children were all fond of music, and also of writing little poems; they loved hymn-singing very much. Each morning the children read their Bibles and prayed by themselves before breakfast. At five in the afternoon, when they had finished their studies, the oldest child at home took the youngest child, the next oldest the next youngest, and so on, two by two, and each pair went to some quiet place, and the elder read a psalm and also a chapter from the New Testament to the other one. They were not to hurry or trifle during this exercise. By all these measures the faithful parents tried to break up bad habits and implant right principles in their family.

When Charles was eight years old he was sent to Westminster School, where his brother Samuel was teaching; John had been going to school some time. John and Charles loved each other very dearly; they had been taught not to dispute with or vex each other, and each year as they grew older they were truer and dearer friends. Charles was very loving and warm-hearted, more excitable than John; John had just as deep feelings, but calmer ways of showing them than Charles.

John and Charles Wesley went to Oxford to college. As I told you in my last story, it was here that Whitefield became acquainted with them. They were pained by the vice and idleness of many of the other students, and they tried to live as becomes Christian people. They were very regular in their duties in college, and, as people who have order or system can do more and in a quieter way than those who are careless and unsteady, they had set times for everything—a *method* for doing things. There were five or six young men who lived in this way, and the other students laughed at them. One day a young man who thought himself very witty called Wesley and his friends *Methodists*, on account of their strict "method" of living. People thought that name very funny, and it has lasted ever since. At first it was given in ridicule, but the people to whom it was given have made it honorable by well-doing, and are not ashamed of it. John and Charles Wesley became the founders of the Methodist Church; there are thousands of Methodist churches and Sunday-schools in this country and in Europe now, and they have done a great deal of good. You must not forget that John and Charles Wesley were the fathers of this great and strong Church. Before this, some plain and pious people who were strict in their religious ways had been called in England Methodists, but only very seldom; but from the Wesleys' time it became the name of a great body of Christians.

While John and Charles were yet in college their dear father died; he was a very holy man. His sons were with him in his last hours. He had always tried to teach them how to live, and now he could teach them how a Christian can die. It made him very happy to know that his dear children feared God and tried to serve him. He said God would take care of his family when he was gone. John said to him, "Dear father, are you near heaven?" He replied joyfully, "*Yes, I am.*" Charles then prayed with him; his father said to him, "Now you have done all I want." Presently John prayed, and while he was praying the good man lifted his hands toward heaven and died.

I told you how poor this good minister was. When he died he was in debt for the rent of his little farm-place and for a few other things. The woman who owned the farm sent a constable and took away the horse, cows and fowls, worth two hundred dollars, to pay for less than half that amount of rent. She did this before Mr. Wesley was buried, while he lay dead in the house. How very cruel! John had been teaching, and he had a little money; he paid the debt and got the stock back, so that it could be sold for what it was worth.

Samuel and some of the sisters were married, and they took care of their mother.

About this time it was proposed in England to send people to America, to Georgia, to build towns and live there. America then belonged to England. Georgia was named after the king, George II. At that time in France and Germany and Ireland were many pious people who were cruelly treated by the Roman Catholics. Georgia was to be a home for these, where they could serve God in peace. As soon as this plan was mentioned people liked it greatly, and money and ships and tools were given to help the people who were going. Ministers and teachers were needed, and John and Charles Wesley were asked to go. John was to preach to the Indians, and Charles was to help the governor and preach to the white people. They were anxious to do all the good they might, and they agreed to go. "Our end was," says John Wesley, "not to avoid want, not to get riches or honor, but just this—to save souls, to live wholly to the glory of God." Was not that a right wish?

Two pious Englishmen went with them as teachers; also some German people, preachers and schoolmasters. On shipboard the Wesleys had to notice the sober and pious conduct of the Germans.

The voyage was a long one. Once there was a terrible storm, and the sailors were in a great fright. The Germans were apart by themselves. John Wesley went to them; he found them calm, praying and singing hymns; the English were screaming. John said to the Germans, "Are you not afraid?" —"We thank God, no," replied several at once.—"But are not the women and children afraid?"—"No," replied the pastor; "our women and children are not afraid to die; they put their trust in God, and he will keep them safe."

At last they reached Georgia, and after a month the two brothers went to different places to preach. Charles remained in Georgia about three years, and John four. The governor did not treat them very kindly; they were sick and often unhappy, and were very glad to get home to England. You know while they were in Georgia the

5

Wesleys sent for George Whitefield, who did so much good in this country.

After the brothers returned to England they both began to preach. They were much in earnest and loved to preach to the poor. They were very good speakers, and crowds came to hear them. Like Mr. Whitefield, they preached everywhere—in streets, from doorsteps and windows, in the fields, wherever people would come. Much fault was found about this; bad men and boys made mobs and tried to interrupt the preaching by noise, throwing stones and fighting. Thousands of people came to these out-of-door meetings, and many were converted. The enemies of the Wesleys did all they could to harm them; the brothers were sometimes knocked down and beaten, and sometimes arrested and taken before judges on the charge of making a riot! All this for just preaching the gospel! Charles Wesley writes that he was "as a sheep among wolves in these fierce mobs; stones flew thick, hitting preacher and people." At one place an angry officer of the army rushed at Charles Wesley, having in his hand a sword with which to stab him. Charles looked him full in the face, saying, "I fear God and honor the king. Strike if you will!" The man dropped his hand, bowed his head and went away in tears.

A piece of ground had been given them to build a house on for preaching. When the house was done a mob came together and tore it down. One day Charles and John Wesley were going to preach; they had with them a young man who loved God and helped them in their meetings. This young man's uncle hated them so that he led some officers to arrest his nephew and make him a soldier against his will. They threw the poor boy in prison, and he was there a week; at the end of that time the judge said he was too short and weak to be a good soldier, and so set him free. The boy went back to the Wesleys as fast as he could. "You were little, like Zaccheus, and that saved you," said Charles. John Slocombe, this boy, was then working in a baker's shop. He grew up to be a preacher, and did a great deal of good in Ireland.

Often the Wesleys preached in the upper

room of some house lent them by their friends. At one time, while Charles was thus preaching, the weight of the people caused the floor to fall through. Down they went, preacher and people, and there was great terror and noise. Hardly anybody was hurt but a large boy of eighteen. I must tell you about him. He was a very bad boy, and he had come to disturb the meeting. He had filled his pockets with stones to throw at Mr. Wesley. When he fell through the floor, with dozens of people on top of him, he was much hurt and thought he should die. He began screaming, "I will be good! I will be good! I will be good!" They took him out and found his leg broken in two places. That was the way he got paid for his bad conduct.

By and by the friends of the Wesleys bought a large building called "the Foundry," and had it made into a church. They built a little dwelling-house next to it, and here their dear mother and two sisters lived until they died.

As years went on the mobs and riots and the hatred to the Wesleys stopped in a great measure. The brothers did so much good, were so gentle and humble, that people were ashamed to quarrel with them. God took their part and made even their foes to be at peace with them.

The friendship of the Wesleys and George Whitefield lasted as long as they lived; they also knew William Wilberforce, a great and good man about whom I shall write my next story; he used to visit at Charles Wesley's house and talk over plans for helping the poor and for building churches and schools. Charles Wesley spent many years of his life in Bristol and London preaching, while John traveled all through England, Scotland, Ireland and Wales. Wherever he went he was the means of doing much good. While these brothers served God thus cheerfully their heavenly Master took care of them. They were never very rich, but they were not so poor as their father, and were able to take care of their mother and sisters.

These brothers loved poetry; they wrote a large number of books and tracts, and hundreds of lovely hymns which I dare say you have often heard sung in church. Charles

Wesley was particularly fond of hymn-writing, and some one describes him thus when he got to be quite old, almost eighty indeed: "He rode out every day on a little horse that was so old that it was gray. He was a very small man, and now that he was old he dressed in winter clothes even in the summer-time. If he happened to think of a good verse for a hymn as he was getting on a horse, he would go on thinking of it and writing it on a little card which he carried for this use in his pocket. Sometimes his first call on entering the house would be, 'Pen and ink! pen and ink!' he was in such a hurry to get his hymn written."

Although John Wesley was five years older than Charles, Charles died first. His brother was very good to him. When Charles was sick, John kept writing to him, telling him to get such and such doctors or remedies. He wrote to Charles's wife, "Never mind the expense; I will pay for all these things if you cannot. We must spare nothing that will help my dearest brother."

But God was about to take Charles Wesley home to heaven; he said he had so many friends there that he wanted to go. His home on earth was a very pleasant one; he had a good wife and daughter and two sons. But in heaven he had Christ his dear Saviour, his father, mother, brother, sisters and several children. Don't you think when he got to heaven it must have been like a real getting home?

John Wesley was away preaching when his dear brother died. Charles sent him his love, and told him to be a father to the children when he was gone. Then he called his wife, and asked her to sit by his bed and write for him a verse which had just come into his mind. Thus he died, an old man, after a very useful and busy life.

John Wesley lived several years longer than Charles. He never thought himself too old to preach; he said when his friends told him it was time for him to rest, " I will rest when I get to heaven. Do you think I travel up and down the country in all sorts of weather for pleasure? No; it is to tell the good news of Jesus to poor unhappy souls that I go, and I will keep on telling that news as long as ever I live."

I will tell you what the old king of England thought of the work of the Wesleys. Charles Wesley had a son who played beautifully on the organ, and he often went to the palace to play for the king. One day he was there, and the king said, " Mr. Wesley, is any one in this room but you and me?" The king was blind. Mr. Wesley replied that no one else was in the room. " I will tell you what I think," said the aged king: " I think that Charles and John Wesley and George Whitefield and Lady Huntingdon have done more for religion and for the good of England than all other people of this day put together."

Thus you see what the Bible says comes true: " Them that honor me I will honor." The Wesleys had endured persecution for Christ's sake, and he gave them their reward both on earth and in heaven.

IV.

THE POOR MAN'S FRIEND:

THE STORY OF WILLIAM WILBERFORCE.

IV.

THE POOR MAN'S FRIEND:

THE STORY OF WILLIAM WILBERFORCE.

JESUS CHRIST is the poor man's friend. He pities, loves and cares for all who need. When Jesus was on earth he was very kind to the poor. The little bag of money which belonged to Jesus and his disciples was often opened to relieve the wants of the unfortunate. He said to his disciples, "Ye have the poor always with you." He meant to leave them as a legacy to the Church, so that people could help them for his sake. He also says, "Inasmuch as ye have done it unto one of the least of these my brethren, ye have done it unto me." Christ takes all deeds done for the poor as if they were done for himself. When the blind beggar by the roadside called to Jesus for help, the Saviour had him come near and be healed. When John sent messengers to Jesus, "the poor have the gospel preached to them" was one of the wonderful works he gave them for a sign. In these days many people scorn and neglect the poor, but many others help them in the wisest and tenderest manner. In the days of Christ on earth the poor had hardly any friend but God. David knew where the poor should go for help; he writes: "This poor man cried, and the Lord heard him, and delivered him out of all his trouble." I think that is a very nice verse for a little child to learn, don't you?

I am now about to tell you the story of a wise and rich man who was the poor man's friend. He had a tender heart; he loved God and he loved the poor. In his care for them he was like our Saviour, who went about doing good.

WILLIAM WILBERFORCE was born at Hull, England. His father was a rich merchant who had many vessels that sailed on the Baltic Sea. William had no brothers; he had three sisters, but two of them died

when they were very young; the other grew
to be a woman, and he loved her very dearly.
Bad boys tease and neglect their sisters; it is
a sign of a coward to do this. Boys who are
unkind to their sisters are the sort of boys
who are afraid of the dark, and who, when
they see the shadow of a tree or post, run,
crying out, "O-h-h!" I don't think much
of that style of boy myself.

William was not a strong boy: he was
very small, often sick, and had weak eyes.
He had, however, a very kind heart and a
wise head. "Wisdom is better than strength,"
Solomon says, and a kind heart is more
precious than beauty or gold. When Wilberforce grew up he used often to say, "I
thank God that I was not born many years
ago, when people thought it not worth while
to try and take care of feeble children. They
would have thought it impossible to make a
man of a poor little fellow like me."

Mrs. Wilberforce was a very tender mother, and she nursed her delicate child so
carefully that by and by he got stronger.
Being so feeble himself made him very
thoughtful for those who were ill. A lady

who often visited his mother said she could never forget how kind he was to the suffering. He would take off his shoes so as to step lightly, and then, going softly to the bed, would say to the sick person, " How are you now ? Can I not do something to make you feel better ?"

When William was seven years old he was able to go to school. Even then he showed great talent for speaking. He had a sweet voice and a good memory, and he spoke so well that the older boys would stand him upon the table and hear him speak pieces to them. The teacher used also often to have him read aloud as an example to the other pupils. When William was nine years old his father died. His uncle, after whom he was named, then took him to bring up. He lived in St. James's Place, London. William was sent to school, but the teaching was very poor. He stayed there two years, going home now and then to see his mother. He had an uncle John who was a good man. This uncle took him one vacation to make a journey. Before they started he gave William some money.

William was surprised to get so much; he said,

"Uncle, this is more than other boys have."

"I give it to you," replied his uncle, "in order that you may learn how to do three things wisely—save wisely, spend wisely, give wisely. Never think that you have a right to use all your money for yourself; the poor have a claim on you that can never be forgotten." This was a good lesson; he never forgot it.

William's aunt loved much to hear White-field preach, and often took the boy with her to listen to that great man's sermons. William took a deep interest in religion; he loved his Bible and desired to live in God's fear. A minister who knew him when he was twelve years old speaks very highly of him as a pious child. His mother and his relations at Hull were moral but not Christian people. They were the sort of folks who called Whitefield and the Wesleys crazy, and when William wrote letters about loving God, keeping the Sabbath and leading holy lives, some of his friends thought he was insane,

and some said he must be going to die. They
alarmed his kind but foolish mother so much
that she went to London to bring William
home, saying that his uncle and aunt would
be the ruin of him. These good people had
no children, and William was like a son
to them; it nearly broke their hearts to
think of having him leave them. He, in
turn, loved them dearly, and felt very sad
to be parted from them. When he got
back to Hull, to his mother's house, he
wrote to his uncle and aunt, "You dear,
good people! I can never forget you. No,
not so long as I live."

He was twelve when he went back to
Hull, and the first object of his friends
there was to take his mind from piety and
make him gay. For the quiet, healthy pleasures of his happy life at his uncle's they now
gave him balls and parties, dances, horse-
races, late suppers, wine, cards, theatres—
everything which should make him forget
religion and become careless of salvation.
Poor foolish people! they did not know the
great sin they were committing. Jesus says
it is better for one to have a big stone fas-

tened to his neck and to be drowned in the middle of the sea than to try and make a little Christian child forget God.

You will wonder why all these temptations did not ruin poor William and make him an idle, godless, wicked young man. The reason is that God took care of his soul. You know what God says to his people: "Neither shall any pluck you out of my hand." Wilberforce wrote afterward about this part of his life, saying, "The religious views which I rejoiced in at Hull remained with me for some time, but my family did all they could to drive them away. I may say that no pious parents ever did more to win to God the soul of a beloved child than my mistaken friends did to drive my soul from him."

William's fine voice for singing and speaking, his love for music and his talent for acting and mimicking, made him very agreeable in company. He had many friends, and they ran after him and flattered him so much that he began to enjoy their society and forgot the truths that he had learned at London. When first they took him to a

theatre they had almost to drag him there
by force, for he thought it wicked to go.
However, at his home and at his new school
there were nothing but fun and frolic and
joking at piety; and by degrees William
neglected his Bible and prayer, remained
away from church, and was as worldly as his
friends, outwardly. But his heart was not at
rest; he often longed for the peace with God
which once had made him so happy, and he
strove to comfort himself by the secret reading of good books and visits to the sick
and poor. He used to think every one was
against him; his relatives tried to make him
worldly; his teachers flattered him to make
him proud; his friends tempted him to be
idle and wasteful. He went to college, and
was much praised for his wit and talent.
As soon as he left he was elected a member
of Parliament. This is a very high office in
England, and in it one can do much harm
or much good. God enabled Wilberforce to
use his place to do good, to aid the poor and
to help the cause of the Lord in all the
world.

He kept his birthday when he became

twenty-one years old in great style. His
friends made a fine feast for all the people
of Hull; they had a dinner out of doors,
an ox roasted whole and a grand rejoicing.
Although he was very rich, he was not ex-
travagant; he had a neat little house near
London, where he used to ask his friends to
come and eat " peas and strawberries." He
thought these much better than wine and
brandy. He gave up card-playing because
he saw it to be wicked, and he no longer
wasted his time at theatres because he had
better ways of spending his hours. He
chose his friends from wise and well-behaved
people. You know there is an old saying,
" A man is known by the company he
keeps." The Bible tells us that " Evil com-
munications corrupt good manners," and also,
" Go not in the way of sinners." We cannot be too careful about avoiding bad company.

One bad habit which he had, of mimicking or making fun of people, was broken up
by a good old friend of his, who said, " Mim-
icry is but a very vulgar accomplishment.
Any fool can turn into ridicule people much

wiser than himself." William saw the jus-
tice of this remark, and gave up a habit
which might have made many people unhappy.

But now, in the midst of his busy life and
his rich friends, God spoke to his soul, recall-
ing him to the love of his early days. He
said to himself, "How dare I live as if I
were never to die? I must prepare to give
account to God." He now withdrew from
those pleasures which kept his heart far
from God, and sought the friendship of
pious people. Worldly persons stared and
wondered because he thought it wrong to
visit on Sunday or to spend time at theatres.
He felt that he needed a pious friend, and
he chose that holy man, the Rev. John
Newton. His mother heard of this, and
wrote, begging him "not to disgrace himself by turning pious"! The good aunt
with whom he had once lived urged him to
seek first of all things the kingdom of God.
Wilberforce now wrote to his mother and
sister, telling them how anxious he was that
they should serve the Lord with him. He
begged them to search the Bible and to pray

to God for help; he also sent them good books and prayed for them. God answered his prayers: this dear mother and sister gave their hearts to God, and now were glad to help Mr. Wilberforce in all his plans for doing good. He wrote to one of his friends, "How can we live as if this world would last for ever? Let us feel that this world is our road to another life, and live so that the life to come will be happy."

In those days English people used to send many ships to Africa to steal or buy the poor negroes for slaves. In these ships the slaves were very cruelly treated, so that hundreds of them died. They were also badly used in the West Indies, where they were sold to work in the sugar, coffee, and indigo-fields. Mr. Wilberforce felt that this trade was a great sin, and he made up his mind to try and stop it. He said to his friends, "The more honor and money and power God gives me, the more I must serve him. I shall use my life, by God's help, in God's service. I shall try and break up the slave-trade; I shall also try and set an example of a more sober and humble style of living. I want Christians to act as if they were not owners of everything, but stewards of God, who must give him an account of all that they do and how they use their money."

Wilberforce's sister was a great help to him. She aided him to build schools and churches; they found time to visit prisons and get homes for orphans. Sometimes his friends told him that he worked too hard; he would answer, "Time is short; Christ bids us work while it is day."

He was often very ill, and always when he got better he would say, "Now I must do more work for God, for I may soon die, and then my opportunities for work will be gone."

Some of his friends called him the "Red-Cross Knight," and said that, like the gallant heroes in old stories, he was always fighting and destroying monsters. The monsters he fought were sins and all kinds of cruelty and injustice. One of his friends used to call his house "Noah's Ark," and said all kinds of creatures swarmed in it; he was so kind he would turn no one away. Widows and or-

phans, sick soldiers, poor men out of work
or in debt, slaves, missionaries, men who
wanted to send Bibles or tracts to those
countries where there are none,—all came
to William Wilberforce. He never got
cross and weary, but kindly heard every
story—gave money, lent money, found work,
advised those who wanted advice, comforted
the sad, and when he was thanked or praised
replied, "This is my Master's work; I love
to do it for Christ's sake."

As you grow up, little reader, you will
often hear William Wilberforce spoken of,
you will often see his name in books. I
want to try and fix an idea of him in your
mind. First, then, remember that he was a
rich and powerful man of England, whose
chief joy was to serve God. His love to
God made him love his fellow-men, and his
tender heart especially turned to all the poor
and troubled who needed his help. He was
a man who used power and honor and money
not to please himself, but to do good. Now
I shall set down in order some of the things
he did, so that you can see how busy and useful his life was, and can connect these good

deeds with his name whenever you see or hear it.

First, then, he fought against the slave-trade in England until it was stopped. Now England does not trade in slaves nor own any. The sin and cruelty that arose from this trade are done away, and Wilberforce was the man who led in this reform.

He aided in establishing the Bible Society, by means of which cheap Bibles have been put in every poor man's reach, and thousands of Bibles have been given away, until now people cannot say they do not have a chance to know the will of God, for his word is everywhere. When you read of the Bible Society, just think that here is a work that William Wilberforce had a hand in.

He was much interested in building schools, not only for children, but night-schools for grown people who had not been able to study when they were young. When wise and good men like Wilberforce set so great a value on education, little children should be careful to improve every opportunity they have for study.

Wilberforce greatly loved and honored the

Sabbath, and not only by his example, but in the making of laws, he tried to stop all labor and vain amusements and parades on God's holy day. He says of Sunday, "Oh what a lovely day, calm, peaceful, sweet, devoted to God! This gives us strength for all the week." You see, children, that good people love the Sabbath, and only naughty folks say, "It is a weariness." If we love God, ought we not to love his day also? It reminds us of him.

There was nothing which Wilberforce hated more than swearing. "Because of swearing," says the Bible, "the land mourneth." Some boys think it is brave to swear; they imagine it makes them manly. They are greatly mistaken. It is a very mean and wicked thing to swear. An old saying is, that Satan baits his hook to catch everybody but the swearer; he will be caught without any bait at all. A boy swears to make himself believed. He does it because he knows in his heart he is a bad fellow and not worth believing. Wilberforce never allowed persons to swear without reproving them. No matter how rich or grand they were, he was not afraid; he would at once reason with them on this subject. He wrote a note to a nobleman who was his friend, asking him to leave off swearing. The nobleman got very angry and sent him a fierce letter, telling him to mind his business: he said, "How dare you reprove me? Here is the book you gave me, Mr. Wilberforce; I will have nothing more to do with you. Send me back the book I gave you in token of friendship; I will no longer be your friend." But Wilberforce sent him back such a gentle, pious, earnest letter that the angry man repented, left off swearing and remained Wilberforce's warmest friend. Let this teach us never to fear to do right or to reprove sin, doing it gently.

Wilberforce aided in establishing religious magazines and newspapers; he was very fond of good reading and highly valued nice books. I hope no little child that I know ever tears up books or breaks off the covers. You are very fortunate in having books to read. Once, little children had no books at all, not even a Bible.

Wilberforce was a great friend to missions. He loved the poor heathen and wanted the

gospel sent to them. He also spent much
time among the prisons, and many good
laws and much kind treatment and teaching
of prisoners in jail were first thought of by
this good man, whose heart seemed large
enough to hold all the world. He was a
man of peace; war he hated. Jesus is the
Prince of peace, and his friends should always try to settle troubles peaceably, not by
war, bloodshed and heart-breaks. Many
boys think war a grand show and that soldiering is a perfectly beautiful thing. Yes,
my dears, it is no doubt very jolly to march
about in gay paper caps with your red drums
and noisy penny whistles. But did you
ever think how terrible is war in earnest,
when sons have to leave their mothers and
fathers their children, and never come back
any more? Did you ever think of the crying there is at home when men are killed in
battle, and how terrible it is for soldiers to
die wounded and far from friends? Wilberforce thought of all these things, and he saw
that there is a glory in peace far greater than
is to be found in war. He was of those of
whom Jesus spoke: "Blessed are the peace-

makers, for they shall be called the children of God."

For all he worked so hard and had begun life as such a feeble baby, Wilberforce lived to be seventy-four years old—that is, as old as your grandfather. His hair grew snow-white and his shoulders were bent, but he had the kind smile coming from a loving heart. He had six children, whom he loved very much. They grew up pious and noble like their father, and were glad to care for him in his old age. Two of his sons were ministers. When Wilberforce was an old man he lost nearly all of his fortune. What do you think he said then? Did he complain and despair because God took away his money? Oh no. He said he was very thankful that God had let him have money until his children were grown up and educated and were taking care of themselves. He could now go with his wife and live with his sons. He also thanked God that he had no debts—that, as the apostle bids us, "He owed no man anything save to love one another." Then he was very glad indeed that he had been able to give so much away. He had made many people happy; had put men in places where they could earn their own living; had helped the sick and built churches and schools and given away Bibles; he had had money long enough to do good with it, and that made him glad. This is what the Bible calls laying up "treasures in heaven, where neither moth nor rust doth corrupt, and where thieves do not break through nor steal." If we thus lay up treasure we will be happy, for Christ tells us, "Where your treasure is, there will your heart be also." The heart of Wilberforce rested in heaven; he sent his treasure there. To him, when he grew old and his work was done, it was not sad to die. No, for his love and his joy were in heaven; Jesus was there; his dear sister had gone there; his daughter Barbara had reached there before him. He was like one who walks along a green and flowery path, picking flowers, hearing birds and thanking God who "makes everything beautiful in its time," and then sees a gate open, and so walks into a lovely garden full of all delight. So, before this child of God the gate of heaven was opened by the Saviour whom he loved, and he went gladly into that happy place.

Learn this verse, find out what it means, and then see if you can live it:

" The path of the just is as the shining light, which shineth more and more unto the perfect day."

V.

THE PRISONER'S FRIEND:

THE STORY OF JOHN HOWARD.

John Howard.

THE PRISONER'S FRIEND:

THE STORY OF JOHN HOWARD.

THE Bible tells us that the Lord hears "the sighing of the prisoners," and Jesus says that those who love him are tender-hearted and visit those who are sick or in prison. There was once a man who was known all over the world as the prisoner's friend and the friend of the sick. Like the Lord, he went about doing good, and I am glad to tell you that his acts did not come just from mere good-nature and amiability, but they grew out of a right principle, a sense of duty, a deep love to God. This man's name was JOHN HOWARD. Howard's father was a very rich merchant in England; he had no children but John.

Mr. Howard had several fine houses in London and in the country, but he kept his little son in the country mostly, because he was not a strong child and city air was bad for him. John sometimes went to school, and sometimes had a tutor at home, but his mother was his best friend and teacher. She was a good, pious mother, and her first wish was that John should be a child of God. She used often to tell him the stories of John the Baptist, of John the disciple whom Jesus loved, and of plenty of good Johns who have lived since, as John Calvin and John Knox, and she would tell her boy that she hoped he would grow up to be like those holy men.

John was a very tender-hearted lad; he pitied all who were in any trouble, was very polite to the servants, and loved much to go with his mother and carry her basket of gifts when she went about among the poor and sick in the village near them.

John was quite a young lad when his mother died; he felt very lonely without her, the more as his father was an odd man, and much away from home, occupied in his business. John had always been an obedient boy and learned the lessons which his teachers set him, but he was not very fond of study. As he was growing up his father said he did not think John would ever make a very good scholar, and therefore he would have him learn a trade. He took him to London and put him with a grocer to learn his business. Some boys love to be in a store; they think it is fine fun to sell tea and sugar and soap and all those sorts of things; but John hated it. Still, he had to stay and make the best of it, since his father said so. He was with the grocer a year, from the age of fifteen to sixteen. At this time his father died. Mr. Howard thought too much money was bad for young men, and he made his will so that John could not have his fortune to do what he pleased with until he was twenty-five years old.

John had got very tired of staying at the grocery, so he talked with the friends in whose care his father had left him, and they said perhaps he had better go and travel on the continent of Europe. He took a good man with him as his teacher and friend. Some young men think they know everything; they do not want any one to tell them what is right or wrong. John Howard was not of this proud spirit; he was humble, and considered it no disgrace to do as the Bible says and "obey those that have the rule over you."

Howard was a pious young man, and when he was traveling he kept his eyes open to see the wrongs and sorrows that were in the world, that he might do something to help those who were suffering. He traveled in Europe about eight years, and then went home to England to get the money which his father had left him.

Not long after this there was a terrible earthquake at Lisbon, a city in Portugal. Do you know what an earthquake is? Perhaps not, for we do not have them in this country; and you ought to be glad of it. An earthquake is a great shaking of the earth; when the shaking is very severe it throws down churches and houses as if they were made of cards; it tears open the ground in great pits, and people and beasts, trees, and even villages, tumble in and are seen no more. When an earthquake is under the sea the water behaves very strangely. The waves rush back and leave dry land where always before they have flowed, and then they rise up like a mountain and roll in far over the towns and fields, where no waves ought ever to come. This is a fearful sight—walls falling, steeples waving like reeds, and people screaming and flying and falling down dead. Indeed, I hope you will never know anything of earthquakes except by reading of them.

The earthquake at Lisbon was most dreadful. A great wave came in, such as I told you of, sweeping all before it, and scarcely anything was left of the once noble city, for the shaken and broken earth and the mountain of water had destroyed all. Hardly a family was to be found without some dead. Children had lost their parents, and parents their children. Those who were left alive had lost their homes, property and clothes; a great cry went up that sounded over all the world. John Howard heard it in London. He could not rest, and he took a great deal of money and clothing with him and set off for the scene of trou-

ble, to see what he could do for the afflict-
ed. At that time all Europe was full of war
and confusion, and the ship in which Howard
sailed was attacked by a war-vessel upon the
sea. The ship was burned, and all aboard of
her were made prisoners and carried to Brest,
a port of France. Brest lies to the north of
the Bay of Biscay. In those days prisoners
of war were very cruelly treated. They were
crowded in close, hot pens not fit for pigs to
be in, and were given hardly any food; besides this, all the money or nice things they
had with them were stolen. Howard and
his fellow-prisoners had a very bad time of
it; some of them died and some got sick.
Howard kept up his courage like a brave
man. If he had been selfish, he would
have thought of nothing but to get free
himself; as he was not selfish and always
lived up to the Golden Rule, he cared as
much for helping his fellow-sufferers as he
did for helping himself.

Do you know what the Golden Rule is? I
will write it down for you, and if you have
never learned it I hope you will do so at
once; then you will be able to tell how

John Howard obeyed it. See, here it is: "Therefore, all things whatsoever ye would that men should do unto you, do ye even so to them; for this is the law and the prophets."

Howard had in England plenty of money and very many friends, and by means of these he at last obtained an exchange of prisoners. The English government gave up as many Frenchmen who were in their prisons as there were Englishmen in prison at Brest, and so many hearts were made glad and the captives were set free and went off rejoicing. We learn sympathy by suffering. If Tommy Brown has ever burnt his finger, he knows how to be sorry for his little sister Jane when she burns herself; Tommy knows how it hurts, you see. So John Howard by having been in prison learned to pity all poor prisoners. He remembered, as the apostle says, "those that are in bonds, as bound with them."

When Howard got back to England he married, and went to live in a fine house which his father had left him in the village of Cardington. When he got to this place it

grieved him much to see how poor the people were—how lazy and dirty, what wretched
hovels they lived in, and how no one cared
for their souls, and there were no schools in
which the children could be taught. He remembered how his mother had cared for
poor people, and he and his wife thought
they would follow her example. He felt
that while wages were so low and houses
were so bad the people had no encourage-
ment to be clean and busy. He went to
work among them with all his heart; he
showed that he was their friend, and as he
was so good to them the poor people tried
to please him. He built neat little houses
and urged each family to have a tidy garden;
he put up a pretty schoolhouse and sent
for teachers; and he had a minister come
and live at Cardington who would visit the
people, preach the gospel and try and lead
them to heaven. In a few years all was
changed. Instead of being a vile, dirty
village, Cardington was one of the busiest
and thriftiest places in all England. The
people were decent and healthful, and everything went well. John Howard, however,

had his own woes; his wife died, and the
only child they had became first sick and
then crazy, and, instead of being able to be
his poor father's comfort, he had to be put in
an asylum. Some people when they have
trouble sit down and mope and fret; others
go to work to do good, and in this way they
find comfort for themselves. Howard was a
Christian, and he found help from God, and
so was able to bear his trials. God is very
tender of his children; he says, "As one
whom his mother comforteth, so will I comfort you." Is not that a sweet verse? During the time that John Howard had been
busy at Cardington he had been also trying
to get the English government to make better rules for the treatment of prisoners taken
in war; he felt that a nation like the English, where Bibles were in every house and
churches in every village, should set an example of doing right and of behaving on
Christian principles. Howard did not believe in revenge; he believed in forgiveness
and kindness.

Now that his wife was dead and his son
gone from him, Howard went again to the

Continent to study the laws regarding prisoners and to see what could be done for the
poor—to educate them and make them more
happy. When he got back to England he
found that he had been made sheriff. It is
part of the duty of a sheriff to look after
the prisons. Howard was very glad of this
office, for he hoped that now he would be
able to do something to make the prisons
more comfortable. He found them damp,
dark, dirty places, where people were herded
together like sheep or cattle. There were no
books for them to read, no work to be done,
no chance to be clean or quiet, no preachers
to visit them. In those days they put men
in jail for debt, as I told you happened to
John Wesley's father, that good man who
by no fault of his own was not able to pay
a little money which he owed. How hard
it must have been for some pious minister or
good father of a happy family to be shut up
in jail in a room with vile drunken men and
wicked swearers who loved nothing but
wickedness! Besides all this there was no
money spent in taking care of the prisons,
and the prisoners had to pay their board

there, and after they were ordered by the
judge to be set free the jailer could keep
them for weeks because they had no money
to pay him.

One of the jails which Howard had
charge of was at Bedford—the very jail
where good John Bunyan was put in prison
for preaching in the name of Jesus, and
where he wrote that dear book, *Pilgrim's
Progress.*

Howard was so distressed by the miseries
of the prisoners that he spent all his time
and a great deal of his money in trying to get
better laws passed and better prisons built.
In only a year he had succeeded in helping
matters a great deal. He had little books or
tracts printed giving the new rules for taking care of prisons, and relating some of the
sad things he had seen in them. He sent
these all over the country, and the English
people felt that it was high time to improve
matters.

As people had now roused up to do better,
Howard traveled in France, Germany, Hol-
land and Belgium, countries of Europe, and
wrote accounts of all their prisons. This

made the kings and rulers of those lands feel that they also ought to improve their prisons; and so all at once half the world began to take an interest in helping to make prisoners more comfortable and to make them better men while they were in jail. Howard said men should not be sent to jail to grow worse, but to make them better; while in prison they should be made to work, to keep clean, to get strong and healthy; and they should be taught their duty to God and man.

You see what, by God's help, one person can do who is only in earnest to work. All the world now loved and respected this man John Howard; kings sent him gifts and letters and asked his advice; and the poor everywhere loved him as their friend. God says, "Him that honoreth me I will honor." Howard honored and loved God, and the Lord made him to be esteemed by all classes of men. A very great orator of England named Burke made a fine speech about Howard and his good deeds. I will set down some of it for you, but perhaps I shall change some of his longest words, so that my small friends will be able to read it easily : "He has gone over all Europe, not to visit the rich, to see fine sights, to please himself, to feast and to dress like a prince; but he went to visit the huts of beggars, to dive deep into dungeons, to visit hospitals, to go wherever there was sorrow or pain. He went to measure, not temples, but human woes, to remember the neglected, to lift up the fallen, to wipe away tears, and to make himself poor—to strip himself of fortune, that he might help the needy." What do you think of that, children? Is not such a life far better than to live at ease and forget the poor? Is it not better than to be a great soldier, and make war and burn cities and rob houses, being called a great conqueror for doing such things?

For ten years Howard gave himself chiefly to improving prisons, and at last all over the world he found new wise laws, and prisons built where comfort, cleanliness and decency were taught, where labor was done, and where people were not put for debts which they could not pay. It is wrong not to pay debts; the Bible tells us to strive to live peaceably with all men, and to owe no man anything, but to love one another. The law now provides some other way of paying debts than to shut up a man where he can earn no money either to take care of his family or pay back what he owes. Don't borrow, children ; only spend money which justly belongs to you. Solomon says, " The borrower is servant to the lender."

At the end of his ten years' labor for prisoners Howard was quite feeble and worn with hard work. He looked sick and old, and more than half his great fortune was gone. Most men would have thought that this was quite enough to do, and would have rested all the rest of their lives. Howard did not feel in this way; he loved to do good. While he had been traveling about to look after prisons he had seen a good deal of hospitals and of what are called lazar-houses— that is, places where lepers or people with the plague are put. The sick were not well cared for in these places. Howard thought that with better nurses and doctors, nicer food, cleaner beds and more air the sick would have less pain and more would get well. He thought so many people ought not to die in the hospitals; and besides, diseases were allowed to spread, plague and cholera and fearful sicknesses were carried from one land to another, because care was not taken of the people who had these diseases or had been among them. To learn their symptoms and the best way of curing them, Howard traveled through France and Italy, and went down into Turkey and the islands of the sea, where diseases are more common than in England. His friends told him that if he went about so among sick folks he would take some bad disease and die. John Howard replied that he was not afraid to die; what he feared most was to live neglecting his duty. He said he did not expose himself to sickness from any idle curiosity or carelessness, but he was trying to do good. He felt sure that God had put it in his heart to labor for him, and that God would preserve him in danger and keep him alive as long as there was work for him to do.

I don't want you to think that John Howard dressed himself up finely and walked about among the sick with his hands in his

pockets. No, indeed; he went to help. He
went with the doctors and nurses to the beds
of the suffering, and he helped to give them
medicine, to bathe their hot heads, to fan them
and comfort them. He took them nice food
and coaxed them to eat, and then he sat by
them talking softly of heaven—of Jesus who
died on the cross for us, and who will not
cast out any who come unto him. Howard
had now so many friends that he soon in-
duced people to care for the sick as they
had done for the prisoners. It was easier,
perhaps, for you know some people will say,
"Serves them right!" when they hear of
persons in prison for doing wrong, while
almost every one will say, "What a pity!"
when they hear of sickness. Howard was
not a man to meddle with things of which
he knew nothing. Though as a boy he had
not loved study, as a man he had learned foreign languages and had studied medicine, so
that he could be of real use to the sick. He
was willing to deny himself both in work,
study and money in order to help others.
In this he followed the example of our
blessed Saviour, who denied himself for our

sakes—for us became poor, in order, as the Bible tells us, that we through his poverty might be rich.

Howard was encouraged to go on with his labors among the sick because he saw how much good he was doing. The poor creatures in the hospitals loved and blessed him, and when he came in at the door there was a smile on all the pale thin faces, and eager hands were held out to welcome him. He was just the right sort of a person to visit the sick; he was cheerful and encouraging, strong and wise and kind. He knew what would be likely to cure people, and he was also able to pray for them. More than that, he could teach them how to die; he could tell them what would make their souls happy. It is a great thing to be ready to die; if we are ready to die, we are surely ready to live. Do you understand me, Katy and Robert? If you are children of Jesus, if you love him and would go to him in glory if you should die to-day, you are also ready to serve him and love him if it pleases him to spare your lives until you are very old and gray-headed—as old as your grandfather.

8

While John Howard was so busy time was not standing still with him; he was getting to be old. He was old, but he did not know it; he was thinking so much of other people that he did not think of himself, and he worked away just as hard as when he was a young man. When he was sixty-three years old he started to go to Turkey, and then into Asia; he meant to go to Egypt, the land where Moses was put in the bulrushes, you know, and then he was going to Palestine, where our Lord Jesus Christ once lived. He was not going merely to see the places, but he wanted to try and help the poor lepers and persons sick of the plague, of whom there are very many in those hot countries, where, I am sorry to say, the people are not very clean. I have seen girls and boys frown, or even cry, because they were made to bathe often and change their clothes. Silly children! Nothing will make them stronger and more active than to be neat; cold water is one of the greatest blessings God has ever sent to man.

Howard accordingly set out from London to go to the East. He traveled slowly, visiting the sick in every city. At last he reached Kherson, a city on the Black Sea. Here many persons were sick of camp-fever, a very terrible disease. Howard began to help nurse the sick as usual, but now, as he was old and feeble, he was more ready to take disease than in his early days. He presently got sick, and a friend who traveled with him saw that he had camp-fever. When the news spread about town every one felt very sad that this great friend of all human beings was suffering so greatly. In a few days the doctors said that he must die. Indeed, Howard knew it before they told him. He was not alarmed; he only said that he was ready, and sent his love and blessing to all his friends. Nearly all his great fortune was gone, spent in doing good; it was treasure laid up in heaven. There was enough left to take care of his poor crazy son. John Howard had all his life trusted in the Lord and worked for him, and his dear Master was near to comfort him in the hour of death. He died very peacefully and happily. He made his friends promise to bury him in Kherson and put only a plain stone at his grave. They obeyed him, and on that stone is a very beautiful inscription in Latin—only three words, but they mean so much: "He lived for others." And did he not live for others? Did he not obey the Golden Rule? I am sure you will all say Yes, yes! The English government put up for him a very beautiful monument in Westminster Abbey, where the greatest men of the land are buried. If ever you go to England you will see it, I suppose.

VI.

THE BOY BY THE ARNO:

THE STORY OF GIROLAMO SAVONAROLA.

THE BOY BY THE ARNO.

THE STORY OF GIROLAMO SAVONAROLA.

THERE is an old proverb which reads thus: "The boy is father of the man." Children puzzle over this sometimes, and end by thinking it one of the queer things grown-up folks say. They ask, "How can a boy be a man's father?" and there they let it drop. You know, boys are often like their fathers, don't you? The boy looks like his father, walks like him, talks like him, acts like him. I think this should make fathers very careful how they behave, when they see that their boys imitate them. As a little mite of a girl said to me this morning, "A body can't write better than their copy."

Now, as a boy acts and is like his father,

so the boy when he grows up acts and is like
he was when a boy. The lazy boy is a lazy
man; a rude, cross, bad boy is a bad man;
and a polite, honest, earnest boy will be a
good and useful man. At least, this is so
often enough to make a rule. It is true that
a bad boy may have his heart changed by
God's grace, and so become a good man; and
some nice boys, forgetting to ask God's help
and keep on doing right, fall away into sin
and go to ruin. This should teach us all to
be careful. The boy whose story I am writing for you in this book fulfilled in his
grown-up days the promises of his childhood.

Far off, in Italy, there is a beautiful city
built on the banks of the river Arno; it is
called Florence. A great many pretty little
girls are named after this Old-World city,
and the name itself is given in remembrance
of flowers. This city is full of beautiful
churches, pictures, palaces, fountains and
images of marble; but, after all, one of its
chief honors is that here lived and died that
good man, GIROLAMO SAVONAROLA. This
name is almost too long to put in a little

book for little people, but don't blame me; you know I cannot help what they named a baby four hundred years ago. Our hero was not born in Florence, but in a city not very far off, called Ferrara. I am sure some of you remember about this city; you read of it in the "True Story Library, No. 2." Don't you know I told you how John Calvin fled there from his foes, and how kind Renée the duchess, the daughter of a French king, lived there and was a defender of God's Church and the friend of all pious people? The father and mother of this boy, Savonarola, were very nice people; they were amiable, learned and rich; they tried to do right as far as they knew; and they were a very happy family. In Italy in those days there was no Church but the Roman Catholic, and to it this household belonged. The mother was rather more pious than the father, and cared more for her Church.

This son of theirs seemed from the time he was a baby to be unusually good and lovable. Like John the Baptist, Jeremiah and Timothy, he was pious from a child.

He was cheerful and kind in his manners, but loved study better than play; he was healthy and always busy, loved to pray and to go to church, and was fond of being by himself, thinking gravely, and of talking to people about heaven and holy persons. In his nursery he used to take the stools, rugs and towels and make little churches and altars and try to dress himself up like a priest. Then he would take a book and pretend to pray, preach and sing. His nurse thought this very wonderful, and she would catch him in her arms and say foolishly, "Oh, you dear, blessed angel! you are too good to live; you will very soon be in heaven, I am sure." This was a very silly idea. God does not take good children right out of the world, as if they were too nice for it, but he lets them live in it to make it better. This boy was especially noted for his love of truth. He hated everything like a lie; he wanted true talk and stories and actions. His first question of anything was, "Is it true?"

His mother looked on him with delight. She would take him in her arms and say, "My darling boy, you shall be a priest or a

monk when you grow up. You will live a
very holy life, and do so many good works
that you will get to heaven. Then after you
are dead you will be made a saint, for your
goodness, by the Church. I hope your piety
will help to save your father and me."

This poor mother knew no better. She
had never heard that we are saved only by
the blood of Jesus—that that blood must
wash away our sins and take us to heaven.
No, she thought people saved themselves and
their friends by their good works, and that
holy men and women might be prayed to
after they were dead. She told her dear
child the best she knew; what a pity that
she knew so little!

His father did not feel as his mother did.
He was glad his boy was good, but he did
not care to have him a priest. He was
proud that his son was so smart and learned
so fast. He would say, " Being a priest or a
monk would be well enough if you were sure
of being made a cardinal or a pope; but such
honor does not come to very many men, and
I am afraid it will not fall to you. So, my
son, you shall be a great lawyer and earn

money and fame, or you shall be a learned teacher like your good grandfather, whom all Italy honored."

The boy made no reply to all these fine plans. In his heart he agreed with his mother and wanted to be a priest. His religious teachers, the priests, encouraged these feelings. I dare say they loved him for his humble manners and his goodness, and they thought he could be happiest and do the most good if he were a monk.

As Savonarola grew up he received many honors and prizes in school for being the best scholar, but little by little he dropped his other studies and cared only for books about religion. If he had had a Bible and such good books as we have in these days, what a blessing they would have been to him!

Thus at home and in school Savonarola spent his early days, like Moses, Samuel, David and Paul, distinguished for wisdom and piety. God meant him to do a great and good work in his life, and he fitted him for it by giving him a fine mind and a tender heart, full of love and fearing to do anything that was wrong.

The terrible wickedness common in those days greatly hurt this youth's feelings; he kept looking about for goodness, and he thought he had found it in an order of monks called the Dominicans. They were really very selfish and exceedingly cruel men, but he did not know this. They pretended to be very pious—to spend their days praying, fasting, teaching the poor, studying good books and nursing the sick. Savonarola thought he should like to live in this way, devoted to good works. He wished he could be a Dominican monk. But his father could not bear this idea; he sometimes laughed and sometimes was angry when his son talked of being a monk. The Bible bids children obey their parents; Savonarola should have been careful to please his father, and not be in too great haste to be a monk against his will. But his teachers, the priests, told him it was his first duty to be a monk, whether his father liked it or not; and as the young man had not been able to read the Bible and learn the will of the Lord for himself, he believed all that they told him.

In those days the Roman Catholic Church was even more wicked than now, for it did not have so many other churches to hinder its bad deeds and put it to shame for vice and cruelty. Savonarola did not know where to fly from so much wickedness except into a Dominican monastery; and perhaps among so much that was bad this was the best. He said he turned monk for the sake of saving his soul. Sin filled him with grief and horror, and the first thing he cared for was to be holy. I wish we all desired it as much. When he was twenty-two years old Savonarola felt as if he could endure his troubles on account of sin no longer, but he must at once be a monk.

As he knew his father would never consent, he made up his mind to run away from home. He took a little book of the Psalms which he loved much, and leaving all else set out on foot one night from Ferrara, and walked to Bologna, where was a monastery of Dominicans. They very gladly took him in and made him one of them. He then wrote a letter to his father and sent it by a servant to Ferrara. He had certainly done very wrong, but he did not know it. His letter is very sweet, loving and pious: I will set down some of it for you to read. He writes thus: "Dear, kind father, I doubt not that you feel sad because I am gone, and all the more sad because I left you without letting you know. But I was sure you would keep me at home, and oh, I could not stay. All the world is so wicked I did not know where in it to find holy men, and I feared to be led into sin and that I would lose my soul. It made my heart ache to see so much sin; I could not endure it any longer. All day my prayer was to God, 'Show me the path in which I should walk, for unto thee do I lift up my soul.' Oh, do not think I went from you in any anger or in pride or foolishness or a whim. No; I went because I wanted to get where I could do nothing but serve Jesus. Dear father, Jesus gave me to you; do you not thank him that he has kept me until now out of much sin, and that he has made me love him—that he has called me to be his soldier? You ought to be glad, but I know you love me so well that you will weep because I am gone. I too

wept all the way here because I must leave
my good parents and my home. But, father,
I have heard the voice of my Lord calling
me, 'Come unto me, all ye that labor and
are heavy-laden: take my yoke upon you
and learn of me, for my yoke is easy and
my burden is light.' I have fled from you
to find rest to my soul. Trust God, and
when we meet in glory we will never part.
Comfort my dear mother, and do send me
your blessing. I will pray for you, my parents, every day. Your loving son.''

Such was his letter. He says he is Christ's
soldier. He was to be this truly—a soldier
who would not love his life, but lay it down
for Jesus. God leads the blind by ways
that they know not; he was thus leading
this young man.

Now Savonarola was in the convent in
Bologna. You will want to know what sort
of a place it was, and how he looked and
lived when he got there. The convent was
called St. Dominic's. It was built of gray
stone, and looked a good deal like a fort. It
had a chapel in it with walls beautifully painted, and many fine pictures hung in the halls

and over the altars. It was divided up into little cells or rooms, each with a heavy door, a narrow window high up near the ceiling, and a small, hard bed against the wall. The floors were all of stone. If you ever go to Bologna you can see it yet. Now it is empty—not a soul lives in it; in Savonarola's time it was full of monks. There was a library in this convent, and in the cellars were the tombs where they buried the dead monks. Here Savonarola found two good men, Sylvester and Dominic, who like himself loved the Lord and wished to serve him. The three were great friends.

Savonarola was fond of reading and study; he loved also to write hymns. Here is a pretty verse from a hymn which he wrote:

"Gentle Jesus, oh how blessed
    He who flies this world for thee !
His the breast whose state is ever
    Calm, serene and spirit-free."

Thus he felt when he got to the cloisters of St. Dominic, thinking he was to live there the rest of his life, calm, studious, holy, happy and loved. But God's thoughts

9

are not as our thoughts, nor his ways as
our ways. This man's cares, strifes and
troubles were all before him. He wore now
the dress of a monk, a black gown tied
about the waist with a rope, to which hung
a cross. On his head he had a black woolen
hood, the cape of which fell over his shoulders. He had sandals on his feet. His
clothes were very coarse. He thought that
he would grow holier if he denied himself
all pleasant things, so he ate no nice food,
only a little that was common, and slept on
a straw mattress laid on a plank. The truth
is, dear children, that God loves to see us all
happy, and is willing that we should enjoy
those comfortable things which he gives us.
But Savonarola did not know this yet. One
great blessing he had at St. Dominic's, and
that was a Bible. Like Martin Luther, he
seized with gladness the dear word of God.
He was one of the teachers of the convent,
and every day, after his teaching-hours were
over, he hurried to his cell and studied the
Bible with all his heart.

He now began to write some sermons; he
spent a great deal of time on them, but did

not preach them. He said he was not holy
enough for a minister. After seven years,
however, he agreed to yield to the wishes of
all the monks and of his friends, and preach.
All the people in the city said that the wise
and holy Savonarola was to preach one of
the wonderful sermons which he had been so
many years in writing, and they crowded to
the great church to listen, ready to praise.
What do you think? Why, when he went
into the pulpit he could not preach at all.
He could not speak well nor loudly, nor remember what he wanted; indeed, every one
was disappointed that a man so good should
have failed in his preaching. He merely said
meekly, " Well, I see that my Lord has not
yet called me to preach the gospel."

For three years more this good man kept
on with his teaching, reading the Bible and
visiting the sick and poor. He was never
idle. He did much good. He was sad because he could not preach, but he was pa-
tient and faithful. At last he was sent for
to preach in the city of Brescia. He heard
in this request the voice of God. He went,
and now indeed he could preach the gospel.

The people hung upon his words; tears flowed over their cheeks at thought of their sins; they longed for that love of God and peace of conscience which the preacher set before them. Now, at once, Savonarola was famous. Hundreds followed to hear him preach. He was invited from one great city to another. All this honor did not make him proud; he only wished to do good. He was made prior or chief of his convent. He still kept his coarse clothes, his humble way of living and his great industry. He clung to his Bible, and taught what he learned in that holy book. He was not only very earnest, very plain and very severe on sin in his preaching, but he was witty and amusing, and knew how to make people remember what he said to them. He loved the poor, calling them " his dear children." At this time he was sent for to become prior of the convent of St. Mark's in the splendid city of Florence. It was a beautiful convent. The prince who built it was a proud and rich man.

When Savonarola got to St. Mark's the monks said to him, " You will have to go and thank the prince for giving you this convent."

"Why?" said he. "Who do you think sent me here—God or man?"

They made no answer. He went on:

"If I have come here only by man's call, I am in the wrong place, and had better go back to Bologna."

"Oh," said the monks, "doubtless God sent you here."

"Then," he replied, "surely I must thank God only, and not any prince."

Lorenzo, this prince, was a very bad man. He did not like the preacher to speak against the sins which he loved. He thought by gifts and by loud praises to hire the pious monk not to condemn his evil conduct. But no; Savonarola felt like the apostles: "We ought to obey God, rather than men."

The pope in those days was named Alexander. He too was very wicked, and he did not like to have the truth preached by the prior of Florence. He thought he would coax him to hold his tongue. He praised him and made him presents, and said,

"These fools of people are not worth your preaching to."

"They have souls to be saved, and it is my duty to teach them all the truth of God," he replied.

"Come, come," said the pope; "don't be obstinate, my friend. You are going a little too far. Talk as the rest of us do. Preach if you will, but preach like other folks. This stuff about the Bible is not meant for stupid people to hear. Obey me and I will give you a cardinal's hat." This was a splendid bribe.

"My lord the pope," replied this good and brave man, "I ask no other or better hat than the martyr's crown."

Those two friends, Sylvester and Dominic, were with him at Florence, and they felt as he did; they were all ready to die for the Lord Jesus.

Savonarola, amid all his cares, honors and dangers, did not forget his early home and his family. He wrote beautiful letters to them, asking them "to live only for sweet Jesus, who calls us to his kingdom." He calls his mother "dearest, most honored and beloved." His sisters and his brother were never out of his mind; he told them that "he prayed for them morning, noon and night."

So great was Savonarola's fame as a preacher that people were willing to walk all night to get a standing-place to hear him in the morning. The people said he was a saint and a prophet; he was so different from all other preachers whom they had heard that they believed him more than a man. His life was so pure, honest and simple, so much above the life of other monks, that they thought he must be an angel in human form. Never had these poor Italians listened to such speaking. People said that to the penitent and humble his words came like gentle dew from the sky, while to the proud and vicious the sermons were like a sword or a fierce storm of hail and lightning.

He was a *reformer*. He wished to make the pope, the priests, the monks and the nuns better; he wanted to bring the Church back to piety and truth. For this the Romish Church hated him, as it hates all the truly pious who protest against its sins. The great men of the Church now resolved to put this good monk to death. He had been eight years preaching, and they would endure him no more.

One evening, while the pious Savonarola and his monks were at prayers in the convent of St. Mark's, a fierce mob led on by priests came to the door. The monks locked and barred it, and with their prior kept on at their prayers. But the cruel mob battered down doors and windows and burned them, and at last got in and seized Savonarola. He begged permission to say some parting words to his monks. The mob let him speak a few moments. He closed by saying, "A Christian life consists in doing good and enduring evil." Sylvester and Dominic were carried off with Savonarola, and all three were put into a dungeon. Here they were kept for more than a month, and were treated all this time with terrible cruelty. The worst things they could do to them only made them call to God, "Lord, receive our spirits." The pope and the priests now made up their minds to kill these three Christians. They

condemned them to be hung and their bodies
to be burned.

On the day of their death their enemies
took off their monks' clothes, saying, "Thus
we strip you of earth and heaven."—"No,"
replied Savonarola; "you may strip us of
earth—we do not care for that—but Jesus
our Lord will surely grant us heaven. We
fear not." They were then led out amid a
great crowd to the public square of Florence;
when they came before the gallows Sylvester
lost all fear and became very happy in his
mind. He turned to his two friends, saying,
"Now is the hour to be firm and to meet
death with a glad face." They then knelt
down and prayed. At once their cruel enemies pushed them from the platform and
killed each one of the three. They then
burned the bodies, and finally gathered up
the ashes of the fire and threw them into the
fair river Arno. Thus, as I hope you remember, the ashes of Wycliffe were thrown
into the Avon and those of Huss into the
Rhine. And, as has been said, the blood
of the martyrs is the seed of the Church.

If you go to Florence now you will see the

convent of St. Mark's, and there they will show you the very dress they took from Savonarola on the day when they killed him, and also two books of sermons and hymns which he wrote with his own hand. These are kept in a glass case, and the writing is quite plain. Thus Florence to-day honors the man whom four hundred years ago she hung and burned and whose ashes she cast away. Here are some verses he wrote:

> " Jesus, refuge of the weary,
>   Object of the spirit's love,
>   Fountain in life's desert dreary,
>   Saviour from the world above!

> " Jesus, would my heart were burning
>   Evermore with love to thee!
>   Would my eyes were ever turning
>   To thy cross of agony!

> " Then, in glory parted never
>   From the blessed Saviour's side,
>   Graven on my heart for ever
>   Be the cross and Crucified."

VII.

ONE OF THE SAINTS:

THE STORY OF LUIGI DE SANCTIS.

VII.

ONE OF THE SAINTS:

THE STORY OF LUIGI DE SANCTIS.

A CROSS the sea, far off from us, on the
other side of the world, is a fair land
called Italy. It is a bright land, full of
fruits and flowers and charming cities. I
think if you could fly over it some day like
little birds, you would say it was a sweet spot,
and that you would like to live there. But
it takes more than sunny skies, green fields
and rich vineyards and gardens to make a
land a happy home. For these many, many
years Italy has been a sad place. It has been
ruled by bad and cruel men; there have been
no free schools; people have been forbidden
to have the Bible, and have even been shut
up in prison for reading it; there have been

hardly any true churches or pious teachers, so the people have grown up in ignorance and sin, and these bring poverty. Thus Italy has been full of suffering and heart-aches. But lately God has been good to this forlorn country; brave men have been rising up to take the power out of the hands of the cruel priests; and I hope by the time that my little readers are men and women the schools and Bibles and freedom that they now have in Italy will have made it as great and happy as any land in the world.

My last story was about a man who lived in Italy long, long ago. Now I am to tell you about a man who lived there very lately, who helped make Italy free, who knew many of the men now living, and who only died about two years since. This man's name was LUIGI DE SANCTIS. What do you think *De Sanctis* means? Why, it means " one of the saints." Do you think that is an odd name? It fitted this man very well. Do you know what a saint is? A saint is a person who loves God and tries to please him. " Saint " means holy. God bids us all to follow after holiness. Those who are washed in the blood of Jesus are saints in glory when they leave this world. Mind now, they are not *angels:* they are better than that; they are *saints.* They sing the new song which angels may not sing—a song to the Lord Jesus: " Thou art worthy, for thou wast slain, and hast redeemed us to God." There is a little hymn you children sing in infant-class; it has a pretty tune, but I don't like it very well. You sing, " I want to be an angel." No, you don't; you want to be saints, saved souls, the children of Jesus; and that is what I hope you will all be. This Luigi de Sanctis about whom I am telling you was truly one of God's saints; he loved and served the Lord in this world, and he has now gone to the world of light, Jerusalem the Golden.

Luigi was born in the great city of Rome in the year 1808. Rome is a very famous city. It is built on seven hills beside the river Tiber. In the days of Jesus Christ people called Rome the queen of the whole earth. It is a very old city. Jesus was never there, neither was the apostle Peter; but Paul was there, and was shut up in prison, and was finally killed just outside of the gate of the city. At Rome are some of the finest churches and pictures and palaces in all the world. People of Italy are very proud of being born in Rome; they think that is a great honor.

Luigi's parents were pretty rich. I am glad of that, and I hope they had a big house, for—what do you think?—they had twenty-four children! Don't you suppose Luigi's mother must have felt like the "old woman who lived in the shoe, who had so many children she didn't know what to do"? It must have been like a party at their house all the time. How did they ever get on with twenty-four boys and girls to be washed and dressed and get their breakfasts every morning, to buy shoes and toys for, to teach their letters, to put to bed, and to fall down stairs and get into trouble generally? Mr. de Sanctis's house must have buzzed like a beehive. What fun! Don't you wish you had all been there to see? I cannot tell you about all these children; some of them are dead, and some are living yet. But I know that one of them was wise and good and gentle, and that one was Luigi.

Luigi's father, having so many children to provide for, made up his mind when each child was little what to do with it. He meant Luigi to be a priest. When the boy was quite small, therefore, he was sent to school to the monks, who were to teach him whatever they thought he ought to know.

The monks had no trouble with their young pupil. He was civil and loving; he minded what was said to him and liked to learn his lessons. The monks put on him a little black robe and cut his hair square about his head; they gave him a string of black beads to say his prayers on, and a little prayer-book with a gilt cross on one side. Luigi counted his prayers by his beads, and when he had begun at the cross and counted all the beads, saying one or more prayers for each until he got to the cross again, he knew his prayers were done. He and some other boys who were to be priests stood up in a ring every night and said their rosary. Some of the boys hurried and laughed or were sleepy and forgot, but Luigi was an earnest boy, and he said his prayers with

10

all his heart. I am glad to tell you that one of these prayers was " Our Father which art in heaven," and I think the boy felt something of what this dear prayer meant, and that God was indeed his Father and was leading him as if by the hand.

The monks taught Luigi to read and to sing, and they also taught him Latin, for in Latin he must read whatever of the Bible he had, and in Latin he must pray, and preach some also when he grew up. As he got older they had him dressed up in various fancy-looking white gowns and red and blue capes and little cornered caps, and he went into church with the priests, and sung prayers and waved censers of perfume about. He thought this was real worship of God, but one day he learned what true religion was.

At last Luigi had finished his studies and was to be made a priest. A good many other young men were made priests at the same time. They all went to a large church one morning, and a great crowd was there to see the sight; among the crowd were Luigi's father and mother, also some of his brothers and sisters, There were prayers and preach-

ing; then the young men, each wearing a long
white robe, marched before a great cardinal
dressed in red and gold who sat on a throne
and had a pair of gilt scissors in his hand.
Each young man knelt before this cardinal,
who took his gilt scissors and cut four locks
of hair from the young man's head. A little
boy standing near caught these locks on a
silver tray. Then the young man, after his
hair was cut, rose up, bowed and went a little
way on one side of the church, where he fell
down on his face, spread out his arms and
lay as if he were dead, until all the young
men were lying thus, and the cardinal rose
from his throne and said a prayer over them.
This ceremony made the young men priests,
and Luigi felt that it was very solemn, and
that now he must be very pious and try to
teach people exactly what was right.

Luigi de Sanctis was so in earnest, so pure
and humble in life, so fond of study and so
kind of heart, that people could not help loving him. He was a man whom God had
made to do a good work, and for this he
had been given noble gifts of mind and
heart. He was a fine speaker and preacher,

and the priests in Rome were quite proud of him. The pope liked him very much, and he was in a fair way to get a great deal of honor and money. But honor and money were not what Luigi de Sanctis cared most for. His heart was set on doing good; the fear of the Lord was his ruling thought.

He preached a while in convents, prisons and hospitals; then he had one of the finest churches in the city of Rome given him, and he was priest there for eight years. After that he was thought to be so wise that they made him chief teacher in the great Catholic college.

Let me tell you now how God led this man to leave the false Church of Rome. The Holy Spirit had filled the heart of Luigi with love to God. Those who love God love the Bible, and De Sanctis said to himself, "The Bible is the word of God; it teaches all the mind and will of God; whatever it says must be right. Of course if my Church, the Church of Rome, is the true Church, it must agree with the Bible. But I know that my Church is the true and holy Church, and so, to be sure, it does agree with the Bible. I shall write a book to show how the Church of Rome and the word of God are exactly alike, and that thus both show and teach the real will of God." Full of this thought, De Sanctis began to write his book. His teachers had always made him study the books of his Church a great deal; he knew very well what was in them. He had never been set to study the Bible much, and what he now needed was to find out what was in the Scripture, and match the Church books to that, just as you would match two spools of thread or sewing-silk. He quietly hunted up an old copy of the Scriptures; it was a dusty, mouldy, dingy old copy, but for him it was to shine like gold and jewels. He read and read and thought, and a great terror filled him and his heart grew sick and ached, for the more he read the Bible the more he found that the Church of Rome has not the mind of God, does not do his holy will and does not teach what is in the Bible. This is what every one finds who studies the Bible and tries to match it with the books of Rome. This is what has brought so many really good men out of that Church—men like Luther and Huss and Calvin and others I have written to you about.

As Luigi de Sanctis was thus reading and thinking, and while he was in great trouble, he had no one to speak to about his trouble. He dared tell none of the other priests; instead of helping him, they would have locked him up in prison. All was dark to him. He asked himself where he should go and what he should do. If his own Church were wrong, was there any Church that taught the truth as it is taught in the Bible and walked in the light of God?

While he was thus unhappy God sent him help; and let me tell you how he sent it. At this time there was in the country of Greece an American missionary whose name was Jonas King. He was a good man. The prophet Jonah in old times did not like to speak the word of the Lord, but the missionary, Jonas King, loved to tell of Jesus; he wanted all the wide world to hear. He wrote a little tract about faith in Jesus Christ, love to God, and the true way to serve him. This tract was printed in a good many languages, and some copies of it were in Italian. A

pious person who was visiting Rome carried
some of these tracts, and one day, being out
walking with a few in his pocket, the stranger slipped one under the front door of Luigi
de Sanctis, the priest of the church of St.
Maddalena. The man who had the tracts
knew nothing of the poor aching heart of
that priest. He just left the little tract and
went away, and never knew that the small
gift would be the very voice of God to a sad
soul. Thus the Bible says, "Blessed are they
which sow beside all waters;" "Cast thy
bread upon the waters, and thou shalt find
it after many days." God says his word is
like the rain and the snow that come down
from heaven, and do not fail of their use, for
they make the earth bring forth and bud, and
furnish bread and corn for men.

The servants in the priest's house could
not read ; they found the " bit of paper"
and carried it to their master's library.
Here the wise professor saw it and read it
through. Here he found the truth; this
was the mind of Jesus; here was the
thought of God's word. The man who
wrote this must belong to the true Church

of God, and this man was what Luigi de Sanctis had been taught to call "a heretic." Anyhow, he was a Christian, and De Sanctis made up his mind to be a heretic too if this were heresy. You know what the apostle Paul cried out to his people : "After the way which ye call heresy, so worship I the God of my fathers."

Luigi de Sanctis now felt that Rome was no place for him. Here, as soon as he spoke his mind and told the truth as it is in Jesus, he would be put in prison. He must go where people were free to think and speak honestly. But oh, how he dreaded to go! He loved every brick and stone in that grand old city of Rome, where he had lived all his life. Here were his friends, here his relations who loved him ; but when once he had left them and become a heretic, they would hate him, and would never be friends to him any more. However, De Sanctis was resolved to give up all for Jesus' sake. He knew the Lord had said, "He that loveth house or lands, or father or mother, or brother or sister, more than me, is not worthy of me." He meant to be able to say like the apostles, "Lo, we have left all and followed thee."

Luigi had two or three friends to whom he dared whisper his new feelings. One of them was Mr. Lowndes, an English gentleman. This friend was to help him get away from Rome. No priest could leave that city without a permission written on a paper called a passport. De Sanctis put all the affairs of his church in order, and asked leave to go to Ancona, a seaport north-east of Rome. No one knew of the change in his feelings, and leave to go was freely given him. He was to travel in the private carriage of Mr. Lowndes. I suppose the other priests thought this was his way of saving expense. Mr. Lowndes knew that Luigi was never to return to Rome or his Church. The two left Rome early on a September morning; the sun was just rising, and the splendid city shone in the early rays. Luigi looked about on all the dear scenes he was leaving, and tears rolled over his face. He shut his eyes, leaned back in the carriage and cried to God to help him to do right. He felt that if God did not give him courage to go he would jump out of the carriage and run back to his friends, his Church and the beloved city, and never follow the truth any more. But Luigi had gone to the Strong for strength, and the Lord helped him. Mr. Lowndes saw De Sanctis weep, and pitied him; he was silent until the carriage was far out of sight of the city, and then he tried to help Luigi think how he was no longer a slave of Rome, but a free man in Christ Jesus. Already, Luigi had told two or three of his best friends how his heart had been changed, and that he meant to forsake his Church because he saw it was false to the Bible. One of these friends was Dr. Gavazzi. Very many of you children have seen Gavazzi; he has just been through this country speaking and preaching. How do I know but some of you gave him money for his dear Italy? and perhaps he took tea at some of your homes, or slept there. If so, you might have asked him about his old friend De Sanctis.

By and by Mr. Lowndes and De Sanctis got to Ancona. There was a ship there bound for the island of Corfu, which lies

off the coast of Turkey. De Sanctis now
wrote a long letter to his chief friend at
Rome, Cardinal Patrizi, telling him that he
should never come back, but had left Rome
to belong entirely to the Lord Jesus. He
also wrote letters to his friends and relations,
and told them how he wished them to divide
his clothes, books and pictures, all of which
he had left behind. He begged them to regard these his last requests, and dispose of
what he had left as honorably as they would
have done if he had died. He left these
letters with Mr. Moore, the English consul
at Ancona, and then he and Mr. Lowndes
sailed for Corfu as fast as they could, so that
none of the priests could overtake them. At
Corfu, Mr. De Sanctis tried to find teaching
or some work by which he might support
himself, but there was nothing there for him
to do. Therefore he again got on a ship and
sailed for the island of Malta, which lies
south of Sicily and belongs to England.
Under the protection of the English government he was safe, for England allows no
man to be persecuted and put in prison on
account of his religion.

At Rome the pope and priests felt both sorry and angry that their wise and good friend had left them; they wanted to get him back. They wrote him a long letter, telling him they loved him dearly; that all Rome wanted to see him back; that if he would only return they would deny him nothing, but would do more for him than he could ask. This must have been a temptation, coming to a poor man who day after day was trying to earn a few shillings at Malta to keep him from being a beggar. He wrote back to his friends at Rome: "I have grieved to part with you, but I left your Church for the safety of my soul; I cannot live a lie. Rome does not allow the pure word of God. I now enjoy a peace I never could find among you. Come join with me if you may; I never will return to you. In answer to all your promises and all your requests for me to return to Rome, I reply, before God who shall judge me at the last day, *I cannot.*"

They said no more to him for almost a year. Then one of the grand cardinals was sent to Malta to talk with him. One day the poor teacher in his shabby coat was walking on the public square of St. George, when he saw coming toward him his old friend Cardinal Ferretti, who had just landed in Malta, arrayed in all his glory. The crowds were admiring the splendid cardinal, who looked as fine as a peacock. How they opened their eyes when he rushed toward the humble teacher De Sanctis, caught him in his arms, kissed him on both cheeks and cried, " My friend ! my dear friend !" Luigi says that after this the people of Malta treated him a great deal better. It did not make him any better, that I can see, to have the cardinal hug and kiss him, but the people of Malta seemed to think it did. This is a very queer world ! Seven days the cardinal stayed in Malta trying to coax or hire Luigi to go back to Rome and be a priest once more. But no, the child of God will not sell his soul for any price—not for all the world.

For five years De Sanctis lived in Malta and Geneva. He spent the time in writing, preaching and teaching. He put all his heart into gospel-work, and of course, then, he was able to do a great deal of good. And what is more worth living for than to do good? While in Malta, Dr. de Sanctis married a nice Scotch lady, who made his home very happy for him and who thought just as he did. He joined the Vaudois (or Waldensian) Church, and that is such a dear and noble Church that some day I must write you a story about it; I should be sorry not to have you know about that people of God.

During these years changes of a good kind had come to Italy. Most of the land was now free, and people could no longer be killed or put in prison for serving God as they thought right. Rome was not so free, but most of the cities were, and among them Florence, the long-ago home of Savonarola. In Florence they had a Waldensian church and college, and a Christian newspaper called *The Echo of the Truth*. That is a very good paper to have in Italy, where the poor people have so long listened to the echoes of lies. Dr. de Sanctis was now invited to come back to Italy and take charge of that newspaper. He was very glad to do so, and went to Florence with his wife and children.

Three years more passed, and then our good Luigi became a teacher in the college. He had taught in a college once before; then he ignorantly taught the errors of Rome, but now he taught the pure religion of Jesus Christ. He was very busy and happy in college teaching the young men, who loved him and looked on him as their father. Only two years of this glad life remained for him. One night he was taken very ill. The sad news went about the college, and the students crowded to their dear master's room. He looked tenderly at them all, but could not speak. Then he turned his face toward his wife and whispered, "The time has come when we two must part." After these words he folded his hands over his breast, and his soul went away to be with the Lord Jesus; from being one of God's saints on earth he had gone to be a happy saint in heaven.

He is buried in Florence, and his friends have set over his grave a beautiful monument of white marble. They treat good men better now in Italy than they did in Savonarola's time, when they burned them and threw their ashes into the Arno. I expect Savonarola was very glad to see De Sanctis when he got to heaven; don't you think so?

One of those who stood by Luigi de Sanctis's grave was Gavazzi. His friend was gone. He looked down on the coffin lying in the grave, and after saying a few words and praying, he cried out with tears, "Luigi, your brother who loved you in exile, and who loved you in our native land from the day you first learned of Jesus, bids you on earth farewell!"

VIII.

A HAPPY LIFE:

STORY OF FREDERICK W. KRUMMACHER.

11

VIII.

A HAPPY LIFE:

STORY OF FREDERICK W. KRUMMACHER.

I AM going to tell you this story of a happy life, because in the first place I know you all want to be happy, and then, in the next place, the person of whom I shall tell you was not happy in any strange or wonderful way—happy in a manner that will be impossible to you; but if you take his method you also can be as happy as he was. He was happy because he was good. Some children, and even grown folks, fancy that good people are dull and sad. Oh what a silly idea! Children who have a good father are happy children, and the children of God have the best of all Fathers, and so, of course, they are happy. Why shouldn't they be? What

I shall write here for you is of course true. All these little stories are true stories; and about this one there can be no mistake, for this man left the history of his life written by himself; he had been so happy that he wanted to leave an account of what God had done for him.

Our hero was named after the king of Prussia, Frederick William IV.; his father was a village minister, and his name was KRUMMACHER. That is a long, hard German name, and you will perhaps find it a trouble to speak it. Never mind; I think you will know it when you see it; you notice it begins with a K. This boy was born on the banks of the river Rhine, the river which all Germans love so well. It was in the time of a great war, when the French were running over Prussia and having everything their own way. Soldiers were in every town, and almost in every house. When the children went into the garden or to school they saw cannon being dragged through the streets and soldiers pacing up and down as sentinels, and often a soldier's funeral, where the dead man was carried

wrapped in the French flag, and all his
friends came after, trailing their guns along
the ground. But all this stir of war did not
disturb the sunny childhood of little Frederick William. All was peace in his home.
Every night the young brothers and sisters
stood about their mother and sung a little
hymn; then they said their prayers and
were safely tucked in their beds. They had
plenty to eat and drink, plenty of clothes
and good kind parents. These children
were brought up to learn their daily lessons
well, to be obedient and to love one another.
After they had worked well they were ready
to play joyously, and as their plays were not
disturbed by loud cries, blows or harsh words,
they went merrily on as long as playtime
lasted. When I see little children who say
they "don't have a good time playing," I
conclude that it is probably their own fault.
They are like the children whom Jesus men-
tions in the Bible, who were never satisfied
with anything. Frederick's father was a
man of a very happy, kindly temper; he
wanted all persons to enjoy themselves. He
taught his children to be thoughtful for

others, and he was also thoughtful for them. Germans are fond of holidays, and usually keep a good many little family-festivals; they did so in this pastor's home. They kept all their birthdays, and the king's birthday too; on these days they made bouquets and wreaths to lay on the table, and had a holiday, a little feast of cakes and fruit and some speeches and songs. They kept New Year's Day also, with visits from their best friends and with good wishes all around, and then they celebrated Christmas with their whole hearts. Christmas was the great day of the year, after all. They had a Christmas tree, with presents for all the family, and they sang hymns about the "Christ Child" who came to earth a little babe lying in a manger.

Besides a good father and a good mother, Frederick William had also to thank God for two good grandmothers, the mothers of his dear parents. These two old ladies were almost the best people that ever were seen. You know in the Bible we read about the boy Timothy who had a good grandmother named Lois, who taught him the Scriptures and who was full of simple faith and earnest love. Such women were these two grand-mothers of Frederick William Krummacher. Of Grandmother Krummacher her minister wrote in this way: " Like a bright star she lights up the sky of her home; she lives in the good sunshine of God's holy truth, and in all her conduct shows a peaceful, childlike, Christian spirit." Should you not think the little children would have loved such a grandmother? I dare say they often visited her, and they could not help remem-bering all the good things she taught them. Frederick William's other grandmother was just as good and lovable; and I don't see that a little boy could be much better off than he was in every way.

The excitement of the great war gradually died out, and while Frederick was learning and growing, from a little child becoming a tall boy, all was quiet. But when he was old enough to be in the grammar school the war broke out once more, and oh, what a stir there was! Boys of fifteen and sixteen wanted to be soldiers; they thought nothing so fine as to march away to battle. Poor fellows! they did not consider what hard times some soldiers have. The Krummacher boys were as wild as all the rest about soldiering; they could hardly attend to their lessons. At their house there were generally several soldiers or officers boarding, and their talk about war and battles stirred up the lads wonderfully. Among those who were at the manse for a while were two, one of whom became a famous surgeon and the other a great general. The one who was afterward a general was quite conceited in his manners, and loved to dress finely and have plenty of perfumery-bottles; the pastor's boys, who lived and dressed plainly, thought this silly and odd, but they found that after all he was wise, brave and witty. Their father told them this would teach them not to judge according to the appearance. The pastor of course would not allow any of his boys to be soldiers. He told them they were too young and must attend to their studies. Out of school they played soldiers and built and captured forts in the garden. They loved to have concerts at home, and learned many songs to sing together; they were also fond of reading, and in the evenings would sit about the table in the little parlor and read aloud. They did not get silly books and run through them once and then throw them aside, but their parents chose for them noble and useful books—histories and grand books of poetry — and they read them through again and again. I wish parents were always more careful what their children have to read. Children should have the right kind of books, and read them a number of times. You need not think I want you to have dull books. I like stories for children, if they are good stories well told ; and I think there are some very nice fairy-tales, and do not even despise Mother Goose; there is a great deal to think about in that book if you only knew it.

Another of the amusements of the Krummacher boys and girls was to act among themselves the scenes they read of in books. They had in their garden a bower covered with vines and fitted with seats, and here they made believe to be all the famous folk they had read of, and acted out the events of their lives. They said that when they grew up to be men they should be soldiers, but I am glad to tell you that when they did finally grow up there was no war—all was peace.   Then, when this peace had come, when the German land was free of its foes once more, the boys had a chance to see how much better peace is than war.   Homes were now full of happy faces; there were no long lists of the killed in the papers, and there was no weeping about the doors of the post-office; whole families came together to the church, and again there were plenty of men to labor in the fields and to follow trades in the towns.   The lads began to see that peace is a blessing from the Lord, and they did not now desire to be men of war.

Frederick William got through his studies at the gymnasium or grammar school with much credit : his teachers praised his diligence, and he entered college with high honor.   About this time his father moved to another home and church; the reason of the change was this : The duke of Anhalt owned the town where they had lived, and the church was under his control.   He was not a Christian man, and he said that Pastor

Krummacher was getting too pious for him! Did you ever hear of such a thing as that? Can anybody be too pious? I think not. In the next place, where Pastor Krummacher went there were some noblemen who were very pious men. They loved God, and were not ashamed to own his name. Frederick William was often invited to their houses, and by their good advice and example he became more thoughtful about his soul and more anxious to lead a holy life. He was going to be a minister like his father, and these good friends often talked to him about what his duties would be, and how he should try hard to get the love of his people, old and young, that he might do their souls good. They told him he must not forget the little children. Jesus loved children; he says, "Take heed that ye despise not one of these little ones;" also, "Suffer little children, and forbid them not to come unto me;" and he said to Peter, "Feed my lambs," meaning children.

Frederick William was now in college, studying very hard. The Bible, however, was the book that he loved the best, and he

studied that the most. By study of the
word of God he " grew in grace and in the
knowledge of God." He chose also among
the students some pious young men who
were his chief friends. These men met
often in a sort of Bible-class to study the
Scriptures, pray and sing together. They
were a very happy little company. By and
by, having studied at Halle and Jena—
places which you can find on the map if
you look carefully—Frederick William was
through his student-life and was made a
minister. Soon after this he went home on
a visit, and preached the next Sunday for
his father. He preached about the miracle
of the loaves and the fishes. Do you remember that? You had better ask your
mother to find it for you in the Bible, that
you may read it. The old pastor liked his
son's sermon very well; after service they
went into the garden and sat down, and the
father gave the young minister some very
good advice. He said: "It is not enough
that you teach what is right to your people;
you must believe it with all your soul. You
must have not only a general idea of the

goodness of God, but you must feel that he is your very Father, and that Christ is your Saviour; and you must have faith in him, that you may be saved." I think this is advice that will be as good for every one as it was for the new-made minister.

Very soon after this Frederick William was called to the fine city of Frankfort-on-the-Main to help the old pastor who had care of the church there. Frankfort is a very delightful city; it has many grand old stories connected with its palaces and castles; the climate is pleasant, and the people are very kind and well-educated. Our friend thought he could not have a better home than this. Besides the pleasure of living in so agreeable a place, Krummacher tells us that in Frankfort he found two great blessings—a wife and a pious friend. The friend was the pastor of a French church in the city; his name was Manuel. He was a very good man, and he and Frederick loved each other like two brothers. Krummacher writes: "I bless the Lord for giving me such a friend. He was my teacher in piety; more than any other man he made me know the evil of my own heart, the power of the gospel and the glories of my Saviour. Oh, the days never to be forgotten which we spent together!" I want you to notice one thing: it is this, that Krummacher takes all his blessings and happiness as free gifts of the Lord, and is thankful for them. He does not feel as if he earned the good things he had, nor as if he had a right to them, but he takes them as the blessings of his Father in heaven. Thus he enjoys them more. We should pray for thankful hearts; God gives us a great deal for which to praise him.

At Frankfort, as I told you, Mr. Krummacher married. His wife was a very pious, happy, loving woman, and she helped him make and keep friends.

Not long after this he was invited to go to a town called Ruhort. His friends said he had better go there, for there was no minister in the place, and he might be the means of doing a deal of good. I must tell you just here that Ruhort and the next two places where God sent Krummacher are among the most pious places in Germany. The people in these villages are famous for their Christian way of life; they make the service of God their chief object. You remember I have told you how poor the father of John Wesley was—that though he was a minister he was sent to jail for debt, and could hardly get food or clothes for his family; and how a cruel person took away all his cattle and fowls to pay the rent. All this was because his people were not pious people, and did not love and honor the servant of the Lord. I wish you now to contrast this conduct with the manners of the pious German people among whom Krummacher lived, and you will see what a beautiful thing religion is—how it softens the heart and makes the life very lovely, and teaches us to act kindly to people. Indeed, I am quite sure you will say that these German people treated their young pastor better than the people in this country generally treat their ministers, and that it is quite a pity that we did not have some of their piety over here. I have known some ministers, especially home-missionaries, who were nearly as badly off as poor Mr. Wesley. I hope that when you boys and girls grow up and have your pockets full of money, you will give a large share of it to

poor ministers who are preaching the gospel
out West, where they get hard fare and very
little pay.

But now I must tell you about Krummacher and his wife when they went to Ruhort. As they neared the town there, float-
ing down the Rhine to meet them was a
beautiful boat trimmed with flowers and
flags, and people in it singing hymns and
songs of welcome. Around this boat were
smaller ones gayly painted and full of smiling people. The big boat held the ministers
from all the churches near Ruhort, and the
little boats had the people from Mr. Krummacher's new church. The large boat took
the young minister and his wife aboard, and
then they merrily sailed up to Ruhort. Here
they found the church and parsonage hung
with flowers, the people making a holiday in
their best clothes and bringing presents. All
this to welcome a servant of God who came
to preach the gospel of our Lord Jesus. Nor
did the people end their kindness with one
day of rejoicing. Mr. Krummacher says:
" They took such good care that our house
was supplied with food that we hardly ever

had to buy meat or drink. They gave us freely of their best. When I said I would plant my garden with vegetables they said no, I must plant it with flowers, which would look the prettiest, for they would send us all the vegetables which we could use; and so, in fact, they did. The kind people kept our birthdays, and came bringing us gifts and flowers; they visited us on all holidays with gladness and singing, and in all ways showed that they deeply loved us."

By and by, when a boy-baby came to the pastor and wanted a deal of milk, as boy-babies have a habit of wanting, these kind people marched up to the pastor's house bringing a fine cow, so that Master Baby could drink and grow as much as he pleased. I think that baby must have had a real jolly time at Ruhort.

Krummacher had here too especial friends who did him much good. You must notice now that he chose his friends not for wisdom or money or high station in this world, but for their piety. One of these chief friends of the minister in Ruhort was a young man who drove horses for baggage-wagons along

12

the river. He was a poor young man, but he loved God, and his pastor was not ashamed to call him a dear friend. I hope you will follow this pastor's example and not be proud. The other particular friend was also very poor; he was a tailor; he had taught himself to read, and the Holy Spirit had entered into his heart and taught him the love of God. I must tell you a little about this tailor. He was quite a wonderful man. People said he was the holiest man in all that country; his face was very mild and beautiful, and he was so gentle, so peaceful, so full of love to God and man, so prayerful and wise, that every one called him " the beloved disciple," after the apostle John. No wonder that the pastor made this man his friend; he said he learned a great deal more from these poor pious people than he did at college. You know James says in the Bible, " Hath not God chosen the poor of this world, rich in faith, and heirs of the kingdom which he hath promised to them that love him ?" Are you surprised that Krummacher calls the years he spent at Ruhort, " sunshine years " ?

From Ruhort he found it needful to go to Barmen. Barmen was even a more pious place than Ruhort; it is called the most godly place in all Germany. Krummacher, of course, did not think the people here without faults; we are none of us perfect in this world. But he found that they tried heartily to serve God, and he says of it that he knew of no place in Prussia where there was so much real, sound piety, and that "it might truly be called one of the streets of Jerusalem blessed above a thousand others." In Barmen and Elberfeld, Mr. Krummacher lived a long while, a great many years indeed, until his little children had grown to be men and women. He says that in these places he does not think there was a house without at least one true Christian in it. He speaks of two brothers who were so tender and unselfish to each other and to all the world that it was said of them that no one ever knew them to say an unkind word or do an unkind deed. He tells us of a carpenter's family who were so generous, so happy and so full of sympathy, that every person in trouble went to them for comfort, and always came away feeling better. He says there was a rich man there who owned a great silk-factory, and who always reminded him of Abraham, because he lived among his people in such a godly, simple and fatherly fashion. He tells of silk-weavers who were so pious in their lives that it seemed as if every day they were just putting the one hundred and twenty-eighth Psalm into deeds, and living it. Do you know that Psalm? Suppose you get your Bible and read it? It begins: "Blessed is every one that feareth the Lord and walketh in his ways."—"Peace was among us," writes the pastor, "and each day I was reminded of the words of Jesus: 'He that loveth me shall be loved of my Father; and I will love him, and will manifest myself unto him.'" While here, Krummacher preached some very famous sermons on Elijah and Elisha, those noble old prophets of Israel, whose history you may read in your Bible in the books of Kings. These sermons were very famous and were put in a book. I suppose you will read them when you grow older. One day the king of Prussia, Frederick William, visited Elberfeld and heard Krummacher preach. He liked the sermon and loved the man. When he went home he wrote for Mr. Krummacher to come and live in the city of Berlin and preach to the king's household every Sabbath. An invitation from a king is the same as a command, and so Krummacher went. Besides, he loved the king very much and was glad to be near him. The king and the pastor were great friends. Krummacher felt very homesick and sad at Berlin, because the people were not as pious as in his dear home at Barmen, but he says this trouble drove him closer to God in prayer. But he soon found many friends among good and great men—men who were wise and pious—and he says that he was very happy then. Indeed, he often tells how easy and happy his whole life was, and he thanks God for it very heartily. He was not happy merely because he was a famous preacher and the friend of the king, for you know he was happy before he was famous or had ever seen the king. He was happy because he served God and chose the children of God for his friends.

One great comfort he had was, that he had never lost any of his five brothers and sisters; they all lived as long as he did, and each time their father's birthday came, even after the old pastor was dead, his children met together as a family to remember and be thankful for their dear parent.

One very prominent feeling in this man was love for his country. He held the German fatherland very dear; he was a true patriot. Krummacher died quite suddenly, but very happily. His daughter says he called his children about him " with a countenance radiant with love and goodness, and if possible even more affectionate than usual." Before many hours had passed his happy life on earth was changed for the happy life in heaven.

IX.

THE SINGER AND SAILOR:

THE STORY OF JOHN NEWTON.

IX.

THE SINGER AND SAILOR:

THE STORY OF JOHN NEWTON.

YOU know I have told you how, when in England there was very little piety or care for religion, God put it into the hearts of George Whitefield and the Wesley brothers to begin earnestly to preach the gospel. A new feeling spread over the land; men began to care for their souls, and parents were more careful to teach their children the fear of the Lord. Among those whose hearts the Lord had thus touched was a woman named Newton. Her husband was a sailor, the captain of a ship which traded in the Mediterranean Sea; he was not a good man, and he was often away from home for months at a time. Mrs. Newton had one only child, a

boy named JOHN. She was very fond of
him, and took care to teach him all the good
she knew. She had him learn early to read,
and she was careful to teach him the Westminster Catechism, which I hope you all
learn. John was a bright boy, and never
forgot what he learned ; the verses of Scripture and the prayers which his good mother
taught him sank deep into his heart, and, for
all he seemed to grow careless of them, they
were as seed that lies hid in the earth, which
by and by grows and shoots up, first a little
green leaf, and then a stalk, and then bears
great ears of corn.

John led an innocent and happy life with
his dear mother until he was almost twelve
years old. Then, alas! that good woman
died, and her child had now no pious friend
and teacher. When Captain Newton came
home after his wife's death he said he did
not know what to do with John unless he
took him to sea with him. John liked this
plan very much. Most boys think it fine
fun to go to sea—they forget the dangers
and hardships—but when they try a sailor's
life they are apt to wish they had remained

at home. You will see how John Newton found that sea-going is anything but easy or amusing.

Captain Newton questioned John about his studies, and thought that he knew quite enough; he was a rough man, and said that " book-learning was of small value anyhow." There was another kind of wisdom which he did not esteem, and that was heavenly wisdom, the fear of the Lord God.

In a short time, accordingly, John set off in the ship with his father. They went south, across the Bay of Biscay, and through the Straits of Gibraltar into the Mediterranean Sea. John had an opportunity of visiting foreign lands and strange cities, and if he had wanted to acquire knowledge he might have learned a good deal. Of course for a long while he was seasick, and suffered a good deal; his father only laughed at him. He was afraid to climb the tall masts and be out on deck in terrible storms, but he was obliged to learn to endure it. The cold, the wet clothes, the close, hot place to sleep, the nights when he was obliged to be on deck and could not sleep at all, were all very hard for him, as was also the coarse sailor's fare which he must learn to eat. But worse than all this was the great wickedness about him. The sailors drank a deal of whisky, and got tipsy and fought; they also swore a great deal, and played cards and cheated each other out of money; so that indeed there was hardly any sin which they did not commit, and they had no fear of God before their eyes. As for the Sabbath, that was not kept at all. At first this wickedness frightened John; he had his Bible and Catechism and a few good books which had been his mother's, and he tried to keep by himself, to read these books and live as he had done at home. He knew his dear mother was in heaven, and he often longed to meet her in that blessed place. His father and the sailors laughed at what they called his piety; they made a mock of his praying and Bible-reading, and said that he would never be half a man.

Little by little John ceased to pray, to read his Bible or keep the Sabbath, and I am sorry to have to tell you that at last he could drink and swear and sing bad songs and be as wicked as the rest.

But you know that God has put within us a voice called conscience. Conscience tells us when we have sinned and warns us when we are about to do wrong; if we commit evil, conscience troubles us and makes us sad. This is what makes the little child who has disobeyed or told a lie so restless and sorrowful. We should always try and listen to this voice in our souls; to go on stubbornly and refuse to forsake and confess our sins when conscience has warned us is called in the Bible "hardening our hearts." Pharaoh, the bad king of Egypt, hardened his heart, and so did Saul, and the end was, you know, that they were quite destroyed.

John Newton had a conscience, and it distressed him on account of his sins. He would think how much happier he had been when he lived honestly as his mother had taught him; he feared he would never see his mother any more—that he would die in sin and not get to heaven; and he felt how grieved his good mother would have been if she had known how bad a boy her dear only son would come to be. After such thoughts John would make up his mind to be better.

Now I must tell you of two errors into which he fell when he tried to reform. The first was, that he tried to be good in his own strength; he did not ask help of God. When we do not get strength from God we are sure to fail, sooner or later. The other mistake that he made was, to suppose he could earn the love of God and get to heaven by certain good works which he would do. He forgot or did not know that we must have faith in the merits of Jesus— that the best we can do is unholy in the sight of God, and we can be saved only by the righteousness of the Saviour. When John Newton made two such great mistakes you may be sure he did not succeed in his efforts to make himself good; after a time he failed. But this trying showed that his conscience was tender, and that the Holy Spirit was speaking to his soul. Once for two years he tried to live a pious life; he left his evil companions and ways, and was, as he says, almost afraid to smile or speak for fear he should commit sin. He had a wrong idea of God and his laws, you see. God likes to have us be happy and smiling, and to use our tongues in a proper way. But poor John Newton was trying to earn heaven for himself, and he had a very hard time of it. After trying so long to be good he fell back into his bad ways; he read a bad book which made him doubt the truth of the Bible, and he grew worse than ever. Of this part of his life he has written this verse :

> "In evil long I took delight,
> Unawed by shame or fear."

In one of his visits to London he became acquainted with a good young woman named Mary. After this he tried to avoid evil ways, fearing this pious girl should dislike him. He said he wished to live so that Mary would not think badly of him after he was dead. He, however, led a very hard life for some time, and finally went to some islands off the coast of Africa, and became servant to a very cruel and evil man who sold slaves to the English ships. This was before Wilberforce had succeeded in inducing the English to stop the slave-trade. In fact, John Newton was so used to seeing black people taken prisoners and sold for

slaves that he really saw no harm in it. He
knew that it was wicked to swear or to be
drunk, but he did not know that it was
wicked to steal and sell human beings. The
truth was, he had been so brought up that he
did not look on black folks as if they had
the feelings of other people, and he did not
know how to treat them. While he lived
on the Plantain Islands he was often very
sick with fever; his master treated him most
cruelly, and he had so few clothes that when
ships stopped there he used to run into the
woods and hide because he was ashamed to
be seen. His only comfort was to take some
books he had and go down to the seashore
by himself and study. He used the hard
white sand for a slate, and drew lessons on it
with his fingers or a long shell.

After some time his father heard where he
was, and sent him word to come home to
England. At first he was ashamed to go,
but he began to think of Mary, and to want
to see her so much that he made up his mind
to go home. He went on board the ship
which had brought his father's letter, but
vessels did not make quick voyages in those

days, and for a whole year the ship sailed along the coast of Africa, getting ivory, gold-dust, ostrich-feathers and spices for a cargo. Then, instead of going to England, it made a trip three months' long to the coast of Newfoundland on the American continent. At last, on the first day of May, they left Newfoundland and sailed for England. On this day John Newton, not knowing what to do with himself, took up a book about Christ to read, and it made him think with shame and grief of his bad life. As usual, he went to bed without any prayer; in the night a furious storm rose, and John was awakened by the noise of huge waves breaking over the vessel; and one of them rushed down the stairs and flooded John's bed, and nearly filled the cabin with water. Every one hurried now to try and save the ship. They pumped the water out and furled the sails, and some cried and some prayed. At first, John Newton was bold and joked, and said he did not care, but the storm rose worse and worse, and he did begin to care a great deal. By and by the captain came near, and John said, " If what we are doing to stop up this

13

leak in the ship does not do, then may the Lord have mercy upon us!" After the captain passed on John began to think, " What mercy can the Lord have for such a bad fellow as I am? The Bible must be true, for my dear mother died happy believing it, and it made her a good woman. Ah, I am indeed not ready to die."

After some days the storm ceased, and the half-wrecked ship went on her way. Solemn thoughts did not leave John; he set himself to call on God for pardon and for help to lead a better life. He beheld Jesus as the Saviour of sinners, and he asked him to be his Saviour and wash away all his sins. Of this he writes in one of his hymns:

> "I saw my sins his blood had spilt,
>   And helped to nail him there;
> A second look he gave, which said,
>   'I freely all forgive;
> This blood is for thy ransom paid;
>   I die that thou mightst live.'"

When at last the vessel reached England, Newton says that he was " a new man, having begun to know that there is a God who hears and answers prayer." After all his

sins and sorrows he was now happy in the
Lord. About these glad days he wrote a
very pretty hymn. Part of it is this:

> " Sweet was the time when first I felt
>   The Saviour's pardoning blood
> Applied to cleanse my soul from guilt,
>   And bring me home to God.
>
> " Soon as the morn the light revealed,
>   His praises tuned my tongue,
> And when the evening shades prevailed,
>   His love was all my song."

John Newton was about as fond of writing
hymns as the two Wesley brothers. He was
a singing Christian. He loved to sing and
to make verses, and he kept on singing the
goodness and grace of God all his life.

John Newton wrote the story of his own
early life and conversion. He said he wanted to show how great is the mercy of God,
who saved so great a sinner as he had been.
He did not try to make himself out one bit
better than he was. He was a humble man.
Some people can never quite own that they
have done wrong, but John Newton was
ready, like St. Paul, to call himself " the
chief of sinners."

After John had visited his father and friends at Liverpool he became mate of a ship sailing to Africa. After the first voyage he was made captain, and then he married his dear Mary. She always had a good influence over him, and made his home very happy. For twelve years John Newton continued to sail from England to Africa; he made a good deal of money, and did not know that he could have any other business. He kept on making hymns and tried to serve God. He had many hours of leisure on board his ship, and these he spent in study. On his return from one of his voyages he was very ill, so that he could not go to sea any more. He then remained on shore, busy in landing goods and seeing to the unloading of vessels. At this time he became acquainted with George Whitefield and the two Wesley brothers, and was a great friend to them. He attended their preachings, and felt as if he would like to become a preacher himself and tell men what the Lord had done for his soul.

He had been so faithful in study that he was fit to be made a minister, and he was sent to a little church in a village called Ol-

ney. He was paid very little—only about
two hundred dollars a year—but he did not
mind that; what he wanted was to preach
the word of God. Olney is not a pretty
place; it is poor and dull, and the worst of
it was that the people did not care for religion. A famous poet named Cowper lived
there, and he was a dear friend of John Newton. Together they wrote a book of hymns
meant for prayer-meetings, and they named
the book from the place, *The Olney Hymns;*
maybe they are in your grandmother's book-
case: I think you will find them in a little
dingy book bound in brown leather. In the
"True Story Library" you know I wrote
you the story of Tom Scott, who wrote a
commentary on the Bible. Do you recol-
lect that I told you he was a minister in Wes-
ton, a village two miles from Olney, and that
he liked to go to hear John Newton preach,
and that he learned from Newton the peace
and truth of God? Newton loved Olney
very much, though other people might think
it dreary. Besides the hymns, Newton wrote
several other books, and many letters to good
people. Perhaps he did even more good by

his writings and his hymn-singing than by his preaching. Very likely you have often heard his hymns sung in church. Do you remember the one beginning, " Glorious things of thee are spoken," or " How sweet the name of Jesus sounds !" or " Come, my soul, thy suit prepare "? All these were written by Newton. It might be a good plan for you to learn some of them.

After John Newton had been some years at Olney he was invited to go to London, to the church at St. Mary's Woolnoth. Here he was very useful and very happy. He wrote no more hymns, but he did a great deal of good. While here he became acquainted with Wilberforce, who visited him to ask his advice, and who learned to love him very much. When Wilberforce was trying to get a law made against the slave-trade he got advice from Newton, who knew so much about it, and he got John Newton to go before the House of Lords and tell all that he knew of the cruelty and danger of that trade. If you will stop to think a little, you will see how many of the great and good men of whom I have written for you knew

John Newton. Let us see if you remember them: John Wesley, Charles Wesley, George Whitefield, Thomas Scott and William Wilberforce. I hope you do not forget what I told you about all of them. The lives of such men are of use to us to set us good examples, and to show us how an honest, earnest spirit may overcome difficulties; also, how much good one man can accomplish who really tries. You must also notice how love to God brings love to man, and how the true Christian makes the world better for his living in it. To John Newton came not only the poor and distressed, but those who were anxious to learn to do God's will. His house was always open, and he never said he was too tired or too busy to listen to the story of troubles and to comfort the sorrowing.

John Newton lived to be a very old man; he was eighty-two. That is a great age. He preached as long as he lived. He grew forgetful as he grew old, so that sometimes, when he was preaching, he would forget what he was talking about, and some one in the pulpit with him would have to remind him what he was preaching about. His friends said to him,

"Mr. Newton, you have preached a great many years, and have done a great deal of good. Suppose that you rest now; you are old and worn with labor." But the brave old man would answer, "No, no; I shall preach just as long as I live. Remember what a wicked youth I was. Shall an old African swearer stop telling of the goodness of his Saviour? Oh no! I owe the Lord all my life, and I mean he shall have it all, every day of it." He was now too old to go abroad much in the streets. He could get to church, and that was about all; but he sat in his easy-chair at home and talked to the crowds of people who came to him for advice or comfort. He was hardly ever alone. The attention shown him did not make him proud. He was called by other people "the true servant and trusty soldier of the Lord Jesus Christ," but in his own eyes he was little and weak. Such a meek, childlike spirit is very dear to God.

By and by this old minister was very ill, so that he could not leave his bed. His nurse and doctor said to him, "Mr. Newton, you are very sick, and you cannot live much longer." He looked up with a smile and said gently, " I am satisfied with all my Lord's will." The Bible says, " I shall be satisfied when I awake in thy likeness;" and so was John Newton when he awoke in the likeness of his Master. We are told that in heaven we shall be like Jesus, because " we shall see him as he is." When Moses talked with God on Mount Sinai his face shone like the sun, and when he got down from the glorious mountain among the people he had to put a veil on his face, because it dazzled the Jews. So those who reach heaven and live in the presence of their dear Saviour will shine like the stars for ever and ever.

You may be sure that John Newton had many sad hours when he thought of his wicked and ill-spent youth. You need none of you feel that you can afford to do wrong when you are young, and that you will "come out all right by and by." Oh no! Suppose you should be cut off in your sins. And then it is not often that a bad boy becomes a good man. We are told, " Remember thy Creator in the days of thy youth." That is the time to serve God. Then we shall not be forced in after years to sit down and weep over the way in which we offended our heavenly Father and led our fellow-creatures into sin.

I have heard of a pious old man who had only given his heart to God when he was old. He used to sit looking very sad, and when friends would say, "Dear sir, what is the matter with you?" he would answer, "Oh, I am thinking how I only gave the dregs of my life to Jesus. Christ died for me, and I only gave the last of my life to him. I waited until I was too old to be of any use in the world, and then I came to Jesus. Oh, I am always thinking of the good I might have done and did not do." When boys and girls came to talk with him this old man would say, "Children, follow Jesus early; don't throw away the best part of your lives serving Satan." I want all my little readers to follow that advice.

I shall now write out for you one of John Newton's hymns, that you may learn it. It tells the sweet story of Jesus' love for sinners—a love that led him to leave the glory that he had with the Father, to become the babe of Bethlehem, a little child in a hum-

ble home in Nazareth, a poor man of sorrows,
acquainted with grief, and finally to die on
the cross of Calvary for our redemption:

> " One there is above all others
> > Well deserves the name of Friend ;
> His is love beyond a brother's,
> > Costly, free, and knows no end.
>
> " Which of all our friends to serve us
> > Could or would have shed his blood ?
> But this Saviour died to have us
> > Reconciled in him to God.
>
> " When he lived on earth abasèd,
> > 'Friend of sinners' was his name ;
> Now, above all glory raisèd,
> > He rejoices in the same.
>
> " Oh for grace our hearts to soften !
> > Teach us, Lord, in truth to love ;
> We, alas ! forget too often
> > What a Friend we have above."

Yes, Jesus is the Friend of sinners, and especially the children's Friend. He himself
said to his disciples, "Suffer the little children to come unto me, and forbid them not :
for of such is the kingdom of God. Verily
I say unto you, Whosoever shall not receive the kingdom of God as a little child,
he shall not enter therein. And he took

them up in his arms, put his hands upon them, and blessed them." Do not fear to go to him with all your little troubles; he is even kinder than a father or a mother. Tell him how hard it is to be good, and ask him to help you. He will surely do it.

X.

A TRUE HERO:

THE STORY OF ROGER MILLER.

X.

A TRUE HERO:

THE STORY OF ROGER MILLER.

ONCE there was a boy in England named ROGER WOODS MILLER. He had a sister and brother older than himself. His mother was not a pious woman, and was also rather idle, and his father was a very bad man. As you may suppose, this family were very poor. The parents never tried to teach their children anything, and at last the father ran away and left his family to starve or get on the best way they could. You would not imagine that a boy left in this way would ever grow up to be a great hero in doing good, would you? But you know the Lord is able to take care of people in any place; and I think he let Roger

Miller have these troubles in his early life in order that he might know how to pity the unhappy, and also know the best way to reach their hearts and homes. Having been so unfortunate himself, he would not be likely to despair of any one. When Roger's father ran away his poor mother put her two boys in the workhouse, because she could not take care of them. Though Roger was only six years old, he was put in the calico-printing works of a Mr. Turner. This was a place where they printed the figures on calico. After a year the masters of the workhouse sent Roger to another factory about ten miles off. Here the owner made Roger work very hard, and was very cruel to him; he hardly got enough to eat, his clothes were rags and he was kept busy all day Sunday. He had no church or school, and was as miserable as a boy could be. This master wanted to get Roger bound to him until he was twenty-one. The poor boy was sharp enough to see that thirteen years of a slavery such as this would be the ruin of him. He had no friend but his mother, and she lived twenty miles off, in Manchester.

If once the papers were made out binding Roger, he could not get away from his master. He made up his mind to run away and get to his mother. Every morning he was sent two miles and a half to bring milk. On the day when he was to be bound he rose early, hid a shirt and a pair of shoes and socks in his milk-pail, and set off as if for milk. The cook laughed and said, " Roger is in a hurry; he wants to get that new suit of clothes and the two shillings the masters of the workhouse are to give him when he is bound."

The little boy, as soon as he was out of sight of the house, hid the pail under a bush and set out at the top of his speed on the road to Manchester. He had had no breakfast, and he was so young and weak that the first day he only got so far as Mr. Turner's print-works, where he had once been hired. Here he met a good-natured workman who knew him, and to this man he told his story. " Poor lad! thee has a hard life," said the man; " sit down and eat this bit of bread and cheese." While Roger was eating the man told him that he would take him into

14

the factory and hide him under a table covered with a blanket, where he could sleep all night, but he must lie very still or the watchman of the factory would find him and turn him out as a thief. Roger promised that he would be perfectly quiet and not be afraid. He was so tired that he slept well, and in the morning the kind man brought him a good warm breakfast and some food to carry with him on his way. The next night he slept in a hayloft, having asked leave of the farmer who owned it. It took the poor boy two days and a half to get to Manchester; there he kept asking after his mother, and by evening found out where she and his sister lived. He made haste to the house, and found his sister sweeping the doorstep. He called her, she looked about, and saw a very dirty and ragged boy standing near. She said, " Who are you, and what do you want here?" Tears ran over his little grimy face as he replied, " Elizabeth, don't you know Roger?" The sister ran into the house shouting, " Mother, here is our Roger. He is not dead; he has come to find us." Word had been sent to his mother that he had left his master, and she thought he was dead, and now was crying within the house.

The mother and sister heard his pitiful story with many tears. They took him in, and the first business was to make him decent. They washed him, cut his hair, and found his clothes so dirty and ragged that they threw them into the fire. His mother then put him in bed, having given him some supper, and went out to buy him some decent clothes. She did not know how needful it is for boys and girls to learn to read and write, and she felt as if she could not live without this poor little lad's earnings; so in a day or two she got him a place in a factory, where he could earn about fifty cents a week. That was small wages and hard work. It was also very dangerous; the children were sickly, and often hurt in the machinery. In those days children worked fourteen hours a day in factories, and hardly any children in the world were so badly off as the English factory-children. Since then better laws have been made; they do not let such young children work, and they have fewer hours, more wages and better rooms. Roger's factory-room was about as bad as a jail for him. Here he toiled until he was ten years old. His sister then married, and his mother went off. He was earning a dollar a week, and had to take care of himself as well as he could with that. One of the first things he did was to find a Sunday-school and church for himself. He had never been taught anything, but he wanted to be able to read. He loved the Sabbath-school very much, and was so diligent and careful that he soon learned to read, and then set about learning to write.

The teaching he received at the Sunday-school kept him from falling into bad habits, and his industry in learning to read and write held him back from idle and wicked company. From the first of his going to Sabbath-school he took a great interest in missions, and said he would love to be a missionary; he had such a pity for the poor and ignorant that he longed to work for them. You know he could tell how they felt from having suffered himself.

When Roger was fourteen he left the factory and went to learn printing, but in three years his master lost his money and his business, and Roger had now nothing to do. He had saved a little money, and he set up a barber-shop. He was tidy and civil, and made out pretty well. You know that barbers often keep their shops open on Sunday. In Manchester, where Roger lived, they always did so, and made more money on that day than on any other. Roger at first kept his shop open like the rest. About this time he was made a teacher in the Sabbath-school where he had been for so many years, and now he felt that it was high time for him to seek the Lord. He thought that if he wanted his pupils to love Jesus he must set them an example; he must be able to tell them "what a dear Saviour he had found." One of the first duties that he thought of performing after his heart had been changed was the keeping of the Sabbath Christ says, "If ye love me, keep my commandments;" and you know one of the commandments is, "Remember the Sabbath day, to keep it holy." Roger made up his mind to keep the Sabbath holy; he told his customers not to come to him on Sunday. This

should have made every one like him better;
and indeed, if this were a made-up story,
you would hear how Roger prospered at once
when he began to do right. But people are
not always rewarded immediately for well-
doing in this world. Trouble was all Roger
got for some time. When he gave out plainly that he would "do none but the Lord's
work on the Lord's day," his customers became angry, and told him that if he would
not wait on them on Sunday they would not
come to him at all. Day after day his trade
became less, and he wondered where he would
get money for his rent. What I am about
to tell you must teach you the great danger
of doing one wrong act, and also that when
we see a duty plainly we should not try to
escape from doing it on the advice of any
one. Roger Miller was very anxious about
his loss of business; the Lord was trying
him to make him a better man; but Roger
got very much discouraged and turned from
the path of duty.

He went one day to talk with a man who
he thought was a Christian, but who really
had very little religion about him. This

man advised him to keep his shop open on Sunday. That was very bad advice, exactly against the Bible. The man said, " You must live. The Lord doesn't mean you to starve or give up an honest trade. Do as other people do. If you don't keep your shop open, some one else will. Folks are bound to be shaved on Sunday; it is a custom. You can keep the shop open Sunday morning, and in the evening you can go to church." This was all very wrong talk. The Bible tells us not to do evil that good may come, and it says, " Trust in the Lord and do good ; so shalt thou dwell in the land, and verily thou shalt be fed." The Bible does not say that we are to keep *part* of the Sabbath holy, but all of it, from the moment when we wake until we fall asleep again at night.

Now I will show you the great danger of disobeying God. Roger Miller listened to the evil advice of his friend. The Bible says, " We ought to obey God rather than man," but Roger in this case obeyed man rather than God. He opened his shop on the Sabbath. He *meant* to shut it in the evening and go to church, perhaps also to Sabbath-

school in the afternoon; but how little do we
know how fast and how far we shall go in a
wrong path! Roger now had about his shop
an idle set of Sabbath-breakers, and with
them he began to go out for frolics on Sunday evenings. Once he had kept a little box
with a hole in the lid, and in this he had
saved part of his money to give to the aid of
missions. But now Roger used up all his
money in folly; he cared nothing for church
or Sabbath-school; he forgot God, and did
not care whether there were any missions
for the poor or not.

One of the first results of his evil life was
that he married a godless young woman who
cared nothing for religion. I shall not tell
you of the next few years of Roger Miller's
history. You may be sure the blessing of
the Lord did not follow him in any way.
The business he had broken the Sabbath to
get did not thrive; he became so poor that
he could not live in Manchester, and he went
to London to look for work. He did very
little better there. He earned but small
wages, and he spent them foolishly; he broke
the Sabbath, never went near a church, and

cared little for his wife and his poor children. These children were running about little, narrow, vile London streets, never going to school, and were as dirty and ragged as children could well be.

Here you must feel ready to despair of Roger Miller; you think that he will die in a ditch. But no; by God's pity he will be brought to repent of his sins and love and live for the Lord Jesus. Still, the consequences of his sins must go after him; people must suffer for wrong-doing; and I shall at once tell you of the punishment of Roger Miller.

His two oldest children were named Thomas and Robert. Before their father became a good man these boys had grown quite large and had learned the worst ways of the city. When Roger wanted to have them do right he found they were set to do wrong. Both of them ran away to sea. Thomas was very wicked, and died in his sins. Robert after a time repented and gave his heart to God. He was wrecked and lost at sea. Thus in his two sons Roger Miller suffered for forsaking "the right way of the Lord."

I will now tell you how after some years of sin and sorrow Roger Miller was led into the paths of peace, out of which he had wandered. One Sunday morning he went off with some bad fellows. His wife was ill at home, but he left her and her babies to get on as well as they could alone. On the way to the river, where they meant to look for a boat, they met a very old lady. She was going to church, and was so old and feeble that she leaned on a cane to aid her slow steps. She looked kindly at the young men and handed them each a tract. Roger took his politely and looked at the title. It was an odd name: *A Wonder in Three Worlds.* When he went home at noon he read it through several times. The "wonder" was the death of the Son of God for man. In the evening Roger stole off alone to a church where a good man whom he knew went. He had not been in a church for years. Tears came in his eyes when he saw this great assembly, all bent on worshiping God. He said to himself, "Do all these people seek the Lord whom I have forgotten? Once I served him too, and sang the Saviour's praise. Now I am a vile outcast, and my poor wife and children are going to ruin by my means." In his soul he began to cry, "Lord, be merciful to me a sinner!" The Lord always hears that prayer. The minister preached on this text: "You hath he quickened who were dead in trespasses and sins." He showed the great mercy of God, who does not cast off any who come to him. "Oh," said Roger, "why did I not remember those words, to take heed lest I fall? I forgot my God, and what a life I have led!"

You know the beautiful story in the Bible —how the Prodigal Son, sick, hungry and far from home, says, "I will arise and go to my father," and how the father sees him far off and has compassion on him, and runs to fall on his neck. So now God had pity on Roger, and he went home that night to begin a new life. The first thing he did was to tell his wife and children of the great change in him. He said to them, "Now I will love you and work for you. You children shall all go to school every day, and to church and Sabbath-school on Sunday; and you too, my wife, must go to church with me."

With tears and smiles all the family promised to do as he said. He left his bad comrades, worked well and hard, and was able to make his family comfortable. The poor wife took courage and kept her house and little ones in order, and before very long she too became a Christian. All the children did well but those two bad boys I told you of, and they were a grief and heartbreak to their parents— the more so that Roger Miller could not help seeing that their ruin was all his own fault, because he had not been a good father to them when they were small.

Now Roger's love of missions and his pity for the sick and sinful returned, and he began to spend his evenings and leisure hours in visiting those who were in trouble and want. He loved Christian work heartily, and he wanted to spend his time in doing the Lord's service. He had so much success that a society for the aid of the poor, called the "London City Mission," engaged him as one of its missionaries. Mrs. Miller was able now to help her husband in his work. They moved into a comfortable little home in that part of the city where Mr. Miller was to work, and while they cared for their children at home all the poor about them were as their children and friends. Mr. Miller preached to the people on street-corners on Sundays; he got the sick taken into hospitals; put the orphans in homes; had day-school, night-school, Sabbath-school and grown people's school; he had singing-classes; he distributed tracts; he found food for the hungry, work for the idle; read the Bible from house to house; and he and his wife had a class where the girls were taught to sew and the boys to be tailors and shoe-makers. Don't you think his hands were full of work? All the poor people loved him dearly; they called him their father, and came to him with all their wants. Every one said that in all London there was not such another able, kind, busy, wise and pious city missionary as good Roger Miller.

One day he gave away five thousand five hundred tracts to a great crowd about a prison-door. He thought a great deal of tracts, because they speak the words of God; and then, you know, one of them was the means of bringing Roger Miller himself

back to the service of God. As you may
think, it needed a deal of courage to go
among some of these people, who hated goodness so much that they hated the missionary
also, and often said they would kill him if
he came near them. They would say this
before they knew him. When once they
found out his kind feelings to them they
would not speak so. I will tell you one or
two little stories of him to show you the life
he led and how he was a true hero. There
were three men living close together who
always treated religious visitors very badly.
These men said that if Mr. Miller came near
them they would throw him into the street.
Mr. Miller resolved to see them. He took
some tracts and a Bible, and some pictures
for the children, and went to their houses
when the men were eating dinner. "Sir, I
hope I do not interrupt you," he said to each,
" but I want to get acquainted with you, and
leave some little books for you to read when
you are lonely. I want also to ask your
children to my Sabbath-school." The men
replied, " You needn't apologize; we know
your feelings are all right, and you are try-

ing to do good. Come and see us whenever you like." Thus, as the Bible says, "his enemies were made to be at peace with him."

There was another man who threatened if ever Mr. Miller came near him to kick him down stairs. Mr. Miller first got his children into school, where they learned to sing some nice hymns, and then coaxed the mother to go to church. The family improved much, and at last Mr. Miller went to see the angry father. The man at once rose and shook hands with him, saying, " I don't know how it is, but my children learn a deal at your school; I would like to visit it. And my wife is much nicer than she used to be." So this man, who was called by the neighbors " the bear," became Roger's friend. I could tell you a hundred stories of this hero, who feared neither fevers nor other diseases, nor evil men, but, like Jesus, went about doing good.

I will now only tell you how he died. His mother, whom he supported at Manchester, died, and he started to go to her funeral. He went on the cars, and some friends were with him. As evening came on they agreed to close the day with devotion. One repeated a few verses of Scripture, another prayed, and then Roger Miller began to sing this verse:

> "Teach me to live that I may dread
> The grave as little as my bed;
> Teach me to die, that so I may
> Rise glorious at the judgment-day."

Just as he sang this the train they were in by some accident crushed into another train, and by the collision seven passengers were killed on the spot. One of these was Roger Miller. He was taken up quite dead. His pockets were full of plans for his ragged schools and notices of church-meetings, with some letters asking help for his hospitals and asylum. He had indeed done with his might whatever his hand found to do, and had worked while the day lasted.

"Blessed is that servant whom his Lord when he cometh shall find so doing."

XI.

THE SUMATRA MISSIONARY:

THE STORY OF HENRY LYMAN.

15

XI.

THE SUMATRA MISSIONARY:

THE STORY OF HENRY LYMAN.

———

MY last story was about a missionary; he was a missionary to the poor in the city of London. This story will be about a man who went to preach to the heathen far away on the island of Sumatra. He was a Yankee boy, born in Northampton, Massachusetts, and his name was HENRY LYMAN. Do you remember that I once wrote you the story of Mr. Brainerd, who was a missionary to the Indians in New Jersey? He was buried here at Northampton. Henry Lyman had pious parents, and a grandmother who loved God very truly and loved to tell the little children about her the story of a Saviour's grace. Though so well brought up, Henry was not a wonderfully good boy; he was very idle, and, being a merry boy, got into mischief often because he thought only of being amused, and did not consider what the consequences of his pranks might be to himself or others. He did not wish to go to college, and teased his father to let him be a clerk in a store or work on a farm. He hated study so very much that he sometimes thought he would run away to sea. The reason he did not run off was that he loved his parents too well to break their hearts. He says he felt very angry because his father made him study, but yet for all that he loved him so much that he made up his mind to persevere for his sake. He also says: "God paid me a thousand times over for my obedience to my parents; all the happiness I have had I found growing up in the path of my duty. God gave me strength to obey, and God repaid me for that obedience." Henry knew how his parents had prayed for him that he might be a child of God, and he *expected* God to hear their prayers and give him a new heart.

Henry had a dear cousin Charles, who

wrote to him and visited him quite often. Charles loved God, and he had a very good influence over Henry. A good example is worth more than silver and gold. When in college Henry was at first called one of the " wild boys," he was so full of frolic and nonsense. But before long the prayers of Henry's friends for him were answered. He was taken very ill and went home; they thought he would die, but he began to get better. Two things happened to him now. One night his elder sister was watching with him. He was asleep, and she knelt down and began to ask God to give him a new heart. She did not speak very loud, but Henry woke up, and in the stillness of the room heard her begging God to give him a new heart. A few days after it was Sabbath and the family went to church, and as Henry was much better they left him lying alone. It was a beautiful day, and as he lay listening to the birds chirping in the trees and to the sweet ringing of church-bells, all the world seemed to tell of the goodness and love of God, and to call him to worship the Creator in the days of his youth.

When Henry got well and went back to college he gave his life to the Lord, who had "brought him back from the gates of death." The Bible tells us that when we love the Saviour old things pass away, and for us all things become new; also, that if any man loves the Lord Jesus Christ he is a new creature. Henry Lyman seemed a new man; he was now all energy and industry, and full of desires to serve God. It was no longer a hard task for him to study: he knew he could use what he learned in Christ's service, and he loved study for the Lord's sake. He was one of those who have one chief wish in this world: that is, to serve God; to this his "eyes looked right on."

One day Lyman and a friend went to visit the grave of Mr. Brainerd. They sat down on the beautiful green grass and talked of that dear missionary. Henry said, "I have often felt as if I must be a missionary too; I believe God wants me to go and tell the heathen of Jesus. It seems so hard that so many of the poor creatures should die without hearing of a Saviour's love!" Soon after this he wrote to his good cousin Charles for advice, and Charles told him to go to the heathen if he felt a love for that work. He wrote to his parents, and they were brave and said yes, they could even give up their dear eldest son to go far across the seas and preach in the name of Jesus. Before long Henry wrote to the Board of Missions, and offered to go and preach to the heathen when his studies were done. He said he would go wherever they would send him.

He now had a dear friend, Mr. Munson, who was also to be a missionary. They were to go together, and the Board of Missions thought they would send them to the islands of Asia. These islands are very hot, but they are very beautiful; sweet spices and rich fruits grow there, and flowers more splendid than we have in lands where winter brings snow each year. But in these lovely lands people worship idols; they are ignorant and cruel; they do not know of Jesus who was born in Bethlehem. To these poor perishing souls Henry Lyman and Mr. Munson were to go. Of course their friends were sad at the thought of parting with these dear young men.

Henry had ever so many little sisters and
brothers, and when he went home for vacation they had the merriest times; he was
such a kind son and brother that he made
his home very happy.   Henry generally
walked home from college, and the day he
was to come some of his brothers would take
the wagon to go and meet him.   Then the little children left at home would climb on the
gate-post and up the old apple tree by the
roadside and watch and watch until the dear
brother was in sight.   Then how they would
jump and shout and clap hands for joy!
The least child of all was sure to be picked
up and have a ride on her brother's shoulder
into the house.   Can you guess how glad
the father and mother were to have their
son home with them?   Then what a good
example he set at home!—always kind and
cheerful, always ready to help.   He weeded
the flower-garden, made boxes and frames
for the flowers, trained the vines and set out
trees.   The children saw how happy their
parents looked when their dear son was
home with them, and it made them anxious
to be like him.   When he was away he

wrote them letters which helped them to be good. Sad enough were the children when these happy vacations came to an end. The big brother went fishing, nutting, berrying and skating with them. He dragged them about on their sleds and made them snow-men. Do you wonder that when he went away they missed him very much?

At last Henry and his friend Munson were through their studies and were ready to go on their mission. They were each married, and their first home was to be at the city of Batavia, on the island of Java. For a whole year their friends had been getting together clothes, stores for housekeeping, books and all such needful things for the missionaries to take away with them. Henry and his wife were home at Mr. Lyman's for the last time. The children made Henry put on the white linen clothes made to wear in the hot country of Java; they wanted to see how he would look; they thought a white hat and white shoes were very funny.

It was June when they started from Boston for the far-off island. The voyage took them one hundred days. They had some

storms and sickness, but, after all, it was a
pleasant time. They made their little room
on shipboard very neat, and had the books,
pictures and other things that had been given
them at home to help make the time pass
cheerfully. By and by they were at Java;
and now I must tell you of the home they
had in Batavia.

They soon got a little house for themselves.
The floors were of brick; it had no fireplace,
no chimney, no cellar and no garret. All
the windows were in front. The walls were
made of bamboo canes, and the roof was
covered with large weeds called *atap* instead
of shingles. There was no glass in the windows. They had iron bars across to keep
thieves out, and wooden shutters to close
when it stormed. There was a long veranda
running all around the house, where it was
pleasant to sit; there was a hall which they
used for a dining-room, and a bedroom on
each side of it. They had also a little room
for a study. They were four miles from the
city, near a splendid park called the King's
Plain. There were many splendid houses
near, and the park was lovely to see.

The island of Java is four hundred and twenty miles from the great peninsula of India. It is six hundred miles long and one hundred miles broad. Ivory, coffee, spices and fruits abound here. It has high mountains and fine valleys; at some places, where there are marshes, it is unhealthy, but for the other part the climate is good. Here our missionaries were to stay while they learned the language spoken in this part of the world, and also the ways of the people. The people of Java are quiet and pleasant, and are not so vicious as many heathen people. Mr. Lyman and his companion-missionary had studied medicine in Boston, and they opened an office where sick people could come for help. While they won the gratitude of the people by curing their sicknesses, they could be also talking to them about their souls and the worship of the true God. They found in Java a missionary from England named Medhurst, who was very kind to them and helped them a great deal. He was like a father to these young strangers in a strange land.

Not long after they had reached Java

there was a ship going to America, and Mr. Lyman sent some presents of curiosities from the country to his brothers and sisters. They were not worth much money, but they showed his loving heart and thought for his friends. I will tell you what he sent: some shells and the teeth of a shark; two nutmegs just picked from the tree, for nutmegs grow in Java; a long pod of cotton, such as the natives stuff their beds and pillows with. He also sent a little idol, shaped like a fat, long-nosed old man, and lying in a small basket; he wanted to show his brothers and sisters what silly things the poor heathen prayed to. Poor creatures! You know they had never learned that commandment, " Thou shalt have no other gods before me," nor that other one, " Thou shalt not bow down thyself to them nor serve them, for I the Lord thy God am a jealous God." No, they had never heard these words, and they bowed down to gods of wood and stone, which " having eyes see not; having ears hear not," nor can understand anything. No wonder that Henry Lyman was sorry for them. Besides these gifts he sent his little sister a tiny wagon made of palm leaves: it was like the carts the native people ride in.

The missionaries were very happy and well in their new home; they were not to have it very long, but they did not know that. They just trusted in the Lord, and lived for him every day as it came. That is a good way to live; if we all took that way there would not be as much fretting. They found very good English friends in this island—a doctor who was very kind to them —and the captains of vessels which stopped there were very friendly; they used to bring the missionaries presents of things brought from America, as hams, butter and apples; these looked like the dear land they had left for ever.

Mr. Lyman loved to go on board the ships and preach to the sailors in English; it seemed nice, so far from home, to find those who understood and used the language of his own country. The missionaries had enough to do—learning the language, helping the sick, visiting the poor, preaching to all who could understand them, writing letters home and teaching in the schools.

The ladies taught the heathen girls sewing and housework when they could get anybody to learn. Mr. Lyman wrote home long accounts of the customs and ways of the Malay people. They are gentle in their manners and have sweet voices for singing; they love to learn and are kind to strangers. They eat with their fingers and sit on mats on the ground. They are very fond of nice things to eat. At one house where Mr. Lyman was asked to tea they all sat on the ground around a table a few inches high; there were no knives, forks or spoons; a servant came and poured water over their hands and gave them a towel. Then they had seven kinds of preserves, with tea, cake and fruit, set before them. In this country they eat their dessert first. Is not that an odd fashion? I should think it would spoil their appetites, shouldn't you? After this fine dessert came the dinner, and they had *seventeen* different kinds of food. I suppose they did not eat very much of any kind. After all were through the meal the servant came around again with water and towels, that they might wash and wipe their hands; and I should think it was very necessary, for they had been eating all this big feast with their fingers—in such a way that if any of you little people tried it your careful mammas would dismiss you from the table; and serve you very right too! However, as you may see, they have different fashions in different countries, and if the Malays had no faults but eating with their fingers, we would not be obliged to send missionaries to them. The trouble with them is that they "know not God, neither his Son Jesus Christ;" and that is a very sad trouble, truly.

Once in a while the missionaries would take long rides over the island to see villages where the people, through the teaching of the Dutch and English missionaries, had become Christians. It was such a lovely sight to see the once heathen people bringing their babies to be baptized and to hear the children in school saying their lessons and singing hymns! Sometimes missionaries from the islands about Java would come to visit them and tell how their work was getting on. The life of a missionary, like all other lives, has in it both pleasure and pain. No one can live in this world without trouble; if we could, I suppose we should never want to go out of it, even to get to heaven. Yet amid all the trouble and care the dear Lord sends all of us much to enjoy.

After six months in Java, Mr. Lyman and Mr. Munson were to leave home for a journey through the islands near, especially to the island of Sumatra. They were to preach where they could, and they were to look out for those places where missionaries should be sent and schools could be opened. They were to be gone six months, and in the mean time the ladies and Mr. Munson's little boy-baby were to stay in their house on the King's Plain. The day they started was Monday; on Sunday evening they had service at their little chapel, and the baby boy was baptized by his father's name. This was a sad parting; six months looked such a long, long while to be away from the dear home. But all these sacrifices must be made for the Lord's sake. The missionaries left their wives in the care of the good friends they had made at Batavia, and sail-ed away for Sumatra.

Sumatra is full of Malays; most of them are pirates, but on shore they are generally kind and quiet. The island is divided into three or four small kingdoms, and one of these is called Batta Land. The island of Sumatra is very beautiful; the breezes that blow from it are full of the perfumes of flowers and spices. A great deal of pepper grows there, and many ships visit the island to get loads of it. The Dutch have some villages and trading-houses along the coast. The missionaries sailed in a Dutch vessel for Padang. The trip was not a very long one, but owing to storms they were two weeks on the sea. They found the people along the coast kind and ready to hear them preach; some of them could read, and were quite glad to get books and tracts in their own language. They found some Dutch missionaries, and learned from them that the people in the central part of Sumatra were very fierce, always at war, hated all white folks, and were as ready to kill men as birds. They were told that Batta Land was full of people; one person said the Battas stood as thick as trees. Now

16

Mr. Lyman felt as if he were truly on missionary ground and had begun his work. Before this he had been where there were many Christians and comforts, but now he was entering wild lands where were only savages.

If Mr. Lyman and Mr. Munson had been older missionaries, and had known more of the Batta people, and of the wars that were then raging among them, and of the dangers of going there just at that time, perhaps they would have waited a while, until a time came when there was more chance of doing the Battas good. As it was, they thought only of doing their duty and of saving souls; duty then seemed to be to go right on in this wild land to persuade the people to have teachers and to tell them of Jesus the Prince of peace. Very often Henry Lyman longed to be back in pleasant Batavia, but he had work to do where he was, and he meant to do it like a Christian man.

The people of Sumatra drank a great deal of liquor; and let me tell you what they called their wine and brandy. They called it *pakor*, which means "nail," and they called it *nail* because they said that every glass of it which a man drank drove one more nail in his coffin; and though this dreadful name all the time reminded them what a horrid poison it was, they kept on drinking, morning, noon and night. You could hear them shouting, "Bring me the white nail!" "Bring me the red nail!" But even here they have felt the good effects of the American Temperance Society, and some of the richest and wisest people in Sumatra, who know what is going on in other lands, have made up their minds not to drive any more of these awful nails into their own coffins, and now set the example of being sober.

The missionaries were warned that they had better keep away from noisy Batta Land just then; war was going on, and the poor savages did not hold any life valuable or know the difference between their friends and their foes. Still, they went on, hoping to be of use, and thinking no one would harm them when they were so peaceable and carried no weapons. They did not yet feel how wicked heathenism makes men. They were not enemies, but friends, and they hoped the Battas would receive them as such.

But, alas! a terrible thing happened. They reached a village called Sacca, and stopped to rest over Sunday. They had just read that verse, "The Lord of hosts is with us, the God of Jacob is our refuge," and that other one, " We are more than conquerors through Him that loved us." They thought of home and friends, and prayed for them; then they sang a hymn. Suddenly from the woods rushed two hundred armed Battas, waving clubs and guns and spears. Mr. Lyman held up his hands to speak, and threw them the hats of his company and some tobacco to show their good-will. Then he gave them the only gun that was in the party. Still the savages pressed on, shouting so loud that they could not hear one word the missionaries said. They shot Henry Lyman and killed Mr. Munson with a sword; then they cut off the head of a servant who was with them.

In one moment it was over; the good

missionaries were gone. Just as they had fairly begun their work they were ruthlessly killed. Henry Lyman was only twenty-four. Oh what a sad loss to the poor wives, to the friends at home, to the Church, and also to the poor Batta people, who had killed their best friends! How sweet it is to know that there is a home in heaven where God's dear children "rest from their labors, and their works do follow them"!

With regard to the missionaries themselves, the case was stripped of much of its gloom. Their habitual preparations for eternity, their known love to the Saviour and their evident interest in the new covenant, made death to them a sudden glory, and the hurried manner of this end only a more rapid translation from labors, travails, sufferings and care to a state of perfect, complete and everlasting rest. We might think that it was a pity that they were not spared to render the Saviour much service in the vineyard on earth. But he doubtless designed them for higher and holier service before the throne above. And with regard to the mission itself, they will not be found, in the great day of account, to have rendered it a partial or an inferior service. The soldier who falls in the forlorn hope, at the storming of a citadel, has as much share in the glory of the conquest as he that divideth the spoil. When the list of worthies is made out, those may stand among the first who nobly dared and cheerfully gave their lives in the good cause.

The names of these devoted missionaries of the cross have passed into the history of missions and of the Church, and are still dear to all who love the Lord Jesus and desire the final triumph of his kingdom. The fall of such men by the hand of violence has not prevented others from filling up the vacant places. Nor ought such providences to deter the youth of our land from entering upon like work. The command "Go ye" still stands in the sacred record. He who gave the command still lives and reigns. He has power sufficient to turn the tide in favor of his cause. And the sure word of prophecy assures us all opposition will in the end prove vain, that the gates of hell shall not prevail against his Church.

Soon the kingdoms of this world shall become the kingdoms of our Lord and of his Christ, and he shall rule over all.

I will now add to this account of these noble men a short extract from a letter written by them to the Missionary Board in this country just after they started on their last voyage of exploration:

"The Lord alone knoweth the future. In him we trust. We weighed anchor at Batavia on Tuesday morning at seven o'clock—just the time, allowing for the difference of longitude, that you were assembled for the monthly concert. We trust the Lord heard your prayers. But we cannot close without inquiring, Are there men preparing to come over and help us? No doubt exists but this people are ready for the reception of the gospel. Send men and Bibles, and pray for the descent of the Holy Spirit, and ere long these great multitudes of people, with their written language and bamboo books, may be reading the word of God and sitting at the feet of Jesus. But send men full of faith and the Holy Spirit; for if they once come among these islands we can assure them they need look for no rest till they find it in heaven."

Will not my young readers seek for something of the spirit of self-sacrifice and devotion to Christ that filled the souls of these men, "of whom the world was not worthy"?

XII.

THE BOY WHO WOULD BE WISE:

THE STORY OF REV. JONAS KING.

Rev. Jonas King, D.D., in Oriental Costume.

Page 251.

XII.

THE BOY WHO WOULD BE WISE.

THE STORY OF REV. JONAS KING.

I HAVE told you children about very many good and great men—men whose examples should make you love goodness and encourage you to persevere in doing right, even though you may have very hard times and have much to discourage you. Some people talk as if they thought little children have no troubles, but I think they have. It is very trying to think you are doing just right, and find you have made a mistake, and to be suddenly reproved as if you were the worst child in the world. Some little people have also other troubles. It is hard to be very poor, and hard not to be able to go to school and learn all that you want to. This story is to be about a boy who succeeded in becoming wise and good because he persevered. He made up his mind as to what he wanted, and then he worked hard until he got it. Like the last story I wrote for you, this is a missionary story.

There are men who have gone over all the world, not to see great cities and lovely pictures, not to visit kings and grand people, not to eat, drink and be merry, but to take the gospel of Jesus to dying souls; to hold up the light of the Bible for those who are in darkness, to make savages gentle and peaceable; to teach parents to take care of their children, and children to honor their parents. These men, wherever they have gone, have done a work which angels watch with joy; they have carried with them the hopes of heaven, and when they have died they have left the world the better for their living in it. One of these missionaries was JONAS KING. He was born at a town called Hawley, in the western part of the State of Massachusetts. His parents were honest, hard-working people; they were too poor to do very much for their children, of whom there were a good many. These parents taught their son to work faithfully at whatever business he had, to speak the truth and not to waste his time. From being so poor he learned to endure hardships, and not to care so much for play as those little children who do not have to work for a living. Jonas went to the district school some, but not much, because he had to be working for the farmers around, as his family needed the few pennies he could earn. He ran errands, planted and dug potatoes, drove the cows to the field, kept the crows out of the corn, led the horses to water, etc.

Thus matters went on until he was fifteen years old; he was now a strong, rough-looking lad, and I suppose the folks about him thought he wanted nothing but to be a farm-laborer all the days of his life. When one learns the alphabet he has the key of all knowledge in his hand. Jonas had learned to read. This sunburnt, barefooted boy felt that there were wonderful treasures of wisdom which he could unlock with the alphabet. He wanted to study, to be a teacher himself some day. He had picked up stray books and papers, and he knew there were very wonderful things in the world if he only could find out about them. He had no one to help him or tell him what to do. It was now cold weather, the fall work was done—the crops were in the barns, the fruit was gathered, the farmers' boys were all going to winter school. Jonas heard that seven miles from Hawley, in the village of Plainfield, there was a schoolmaster named Maynard who was very anxious to have his pupils learn, and who talked much to the boys about getting an education. Jonas heard that Mr. Maynard had said that any boy could become a wise man who really desired it. He said to himself, "I desire it; let me see if I can be a wise man. I will go and talk with Mr. Maynard."

One frosty morning he rose early and set out on his seven-miles walk to visit the schoolmaster at Plainfield. He tied his red woolen scarf about his neck and thrust his hands in his pockets to keep them warm, and off he trudged bravely. The wind blew in his face sharply, the snow lay on the ground, but he walked fast to keep himself warm, and before school-time he reached the little log school-house at Plainfield. The children were standing about the yard and in the school-room. They all looked curiously at the strange boy. "Who is it?" they whispered among themselves. One boy said, " I know; his name is Jonas, and he works over in Hawley. What do you think he wants here?" Nobody could tell, and they all stared the harder.

By and by Mr. Maynard came in, and he saw the new boy sitting behind the stove getting warm. He walked up and shook hands with the stranger, asking pleasantly, " What is your name, lad?"

" It is Jonas King, sir."

" And what do you want, my lad? Do you live near here?"

" No, sir; I live seven miles off, in Hawley. What I want is to get an education. I'm fifteen years old, sir, and I have no time to lose. I must begin right away."

" Very good, my boy; and how much do you know now?"

" Well, I can read and write, and cipher some, sir."

" Have you any friends who are able to help you ?"

Jonas shook his head.

" And are not your parents able to do anything for you ?"

" No, sir," replied Jonas. " If I can get them to let me have my time, that is all I can look for ; they are very poor indeed."

" How, then, my son, do you expect to support yourself and get an education ?" asked Mr. Maynard.

" I'm going to try with all my might, and work like anything," replied Jonas sturdily. " I came here because I thought you could tell me how to set about it. I don't know where I ought to go or what I should study first. Can't you tell me something, Mr. Maynard ?"

Yes, Mr. Maynard said he would help him. He advised Jonas to stay there in school that day, and study with the other boys, and by evening he would see what he could do for him. So he gave him some books, and then school began.

Mr. Maynard says that he did not find Jonas King remarkably bright or intelligent, but he found out at once that he was industrious and persevering. This is better than to be smart. Get some one to tell you the story of the Hare and the Tortoise, and then you will understand what I mean by this.

Mr. Maynard especially noticed the calm, earnest manner with which Jonas King met difficulties which would have made most boys or men faint-hearted. With no books, no money to pay his board, no stock of warm clothes, here in the beginning of winter he was ready to undertake to support himself through years of study. Mr. Maynard said, "This boy will succeed, because he makes up his mind and then goes right on."

At noon Mr. Maynard went home to his boarding-house and told there the story of Jonas King. The master of the house said he came of an honest family, and after a little talk concluded to give Jonas his board during the winter for the work he could do out of school-hours. This was a grand thing for Jonas, for he could study in the evening, and Mr. Maynard would be right there in the house to help him.

17

After school Mr. Maynard told Jonas what he had done for him, and Jonas was very thankful. The teacher said he could find him enough books that some of the richer boys were done with. Jonas had hard work to do, but he was willing to do it. He made fires, cut the wood, milked the cows, brought water, helped the servant-woman in many ways, and was always ready cheerfully to do errands for any one. Everybody liked him because he was so faithful. He made himself respected by his good conduct. People said, "That Jonas King will make a man of himself in spite of every difficulty." Such a boy could always get work. He rose early and worked rapidly, and often had some hours to spare on Saturday, when the people he boarded with did not need him, and then he would get work at corn-husking and wood-sawing among the neighbors, and thus he was able to earn his clothes.

The minister at Plainfield soon took a great interest in Jonas. The boy was regularly at church and Sabbath-school, and gave attention to all that was said. A lad cannot do better than make a friend of his minister; and this is what Jonas did.

In the spring, kind Mr. Maynard left Plainfield. Mr. Hallock, the minister, then said Jonas should come and live with him, work for him in house and garden, and study with him until he was ready for college. Jonas was very thankful for this offer. Mr. Hallock was a dear old gentleman; he loved to teach boys, and at different times he had a great many under his care. The young men would come to Plainfield and board, study with the old pastor until they were ready for college, and then, with his blessing and prayers, would go off together to college. One of these students was Jonas King. Perhaps no one of the pupils of Mr. Hallock was more steady and persevering than this young man, who was to become a great blessing to the world. Jonas was nineteen when he entered college, and he was there four years. The president and professors loved him very much for his sound Christian principles, his amiable manners and his humble, industrious habits. From college Jonas King went to the theo-

logical seminary; and I must tell you that
of the class he belonged to six were missionaries.   There was a good deal of missionary
spirit in that class; don't you think so?
While here, and for two years afterward,
Jonas King showed a great genius for learning the languages of the East—of the land
where Jesus lived, and the country of the
Arabs, and of India.   There are many
books in these languages, and the Bible
was first written in Hebrew and in Greek;
so people learn these tongues still.   Mr.
King was invited to go to a new college and
teach these languages.   Being a very modest
man, he said that he did not feel that he
knew quite enough to teach these studies
yet, and he would like to go to France and
learn a little more.   He had now some very
rich friends who had learned to care very
much for him, and they approved so highly
of his going to France that they gave him
all the money he needed.   He went to the
city of Paris, and began to study with all
his might.   He had not been there long
when he heard of the death of a missionary
named Parsons, who had gone to Palestine

to preach the gospel. Mr. Parsons had gone out with a Mr. Fisk, and now Mr. Fisk was in great need of some other missionary to come out and help him—some one who could speak Arabic and travel about with him to establish churches and schools.

Some friends wrote to Mr. Fisk about Jonas King, then in Paris, saying that they thought he would be just the right man, and that as Mr. King loved to do good and had often spoken of being a missionary, they thought he could be persuaded to go to Palestine. Mr. Fisk wrote right away to Jonas King, begging him to come and help him. He told how sad and lonely it was for him without his dear friend and helper, and how terrible to see heathen in the lovely land where David had written the Psalms, Elijah had gone to heaven in a whirlwind with a chariot of fire, John the Baptist had preached, Stephen had been killed, and the Saviour of the world had been born and lived, died and risen again, and gone up into heaven. Who would not love and pity this land? Would not Mr. King go at once to work where Christ and his apostles had labored years ago?

Yes, the heart of Jonas King was ready for this work. He called together his friends and laid the case before them. They told him to go, and promised money for the mission so long as he should be there. Some of his friends said, "Traveling in the East is not very safe, and the climate is bad for strangers; you may lose your life going there." He replied—and it was a noble answer—"All about me here in Paris I see soldiers who are ready to go anywhere, into any danger, and fight for the king of France. I see soldiers in the streets and hospitals who have lost an arm, an eye or a leg fighting for a little earthly glory, and shall I hesitate to go out and risk my life in the service of the Prince of peace, who will give me a crown of immortal life when my work on earth is done?"

Mr. King had a very delightful journey through France. He sailed from Marseilles on a beautiful October day. He reached the island of Malta in a few days, and there he found Mr. Fisk waiting for him. They

next sailed to Alexandria, a city in Egypt;
going here, they passed the delightful land
of Greece, where Mr. King was to spend
many useful and happy years; people are
generally happy when they are doing good.
Our missionaries were in Egypt three months.
You may know how busy they were if I tell
you that they distributed nine hundred Bibles
three thousand tracts printed in twelve different languages, and along with another missionary, named Wolff, they preached the gospel speaking in seven different languages.
This was doing a good deal of work; don't
you think so? That is the kind of men
we have for missionaries. I hope you will
always love and respect them, and do all
you can to help them in their grand, good
work.

Now they were to cross the desert to go to
Palestine, the land called Canaan in the Bible. How many stories you have read about
it! Here David killed Goliath; here the
walls of Jericho fell down; here lived Sam-
son the strong and Solomon the wise. Oh,
what a wonderful old land it is! The desert
is a trying place to travel over; it is hot like

an oven; the winds are almost as if they blew to you off from a fire; then water is very scarce, and it has to be carried in leather bottles, because there are no wells to stop at for a drink; the leather makes the water dark and ill-tasted and warm; I know you wouldn't like to drink it. Mr. King and Mr. Fisk traveled on camels; did you ever see a camel? They got quite out of water, and had a deal of trouble.

I will tell you how they spent one evening of the journey. When they stopped for the night they unloaded the camels and set up their tents. Then they had some supper. Many people were traveling with them. One was a Persian named Mohammed; he was quite a wise man, and was called a dervish. After supper the missionaries took some Bibles in Persian and Arabic and went to him to read them, so that they might learn the languages better. They carried a square piece of carpet, and laid it on the sand near the dervish. Then they began to read to him, and very many of the other travelers came around and sat down to listen. When they heard some chapters from Genesis, the first book in the Bible, read, they said it was very good. Another cried out, "No, it is not good; it is an *infidel* book." Pretty soon one of the servants, named Elias, became very angry with his mother, who was cooking his supper. He struck her! What a wicked man, to do this! Mr. Wolff went to him and reproved him. Some of the Arabs cried out, "Let him alone; he is bad because he is a *Christian*." They hate Christians. Mr. Wolff made Elias ashamed of his ill-conduct. He went to his mother, took her hand and kissed it, and said he would never strike her again. Before long two Turks began to fight, and the missionaries had to stop them; and soon after a Persian got very angry with a poor little donkey, and began, like Balaam, to beat him, ending by calling the poor beast *a Jew.* Thus you see these people are very quarrelsome, and hate Jews and Christians and everybody but themselves. How much they need to learn of the principles of that pure religion which comes from above, the *peaceable* religion!

Mr. King was in Palestine three years.

He was much interested in the Armenian people, and when he reached France on his way home he got them a printing-press and some types and sent them to Palestine, so that books in their own language could be provided for them.

Mr. King was only in America a year, and during that time he was busy collecting money for missions. Then he was invited to go to the land of Greece. A ship was to be sent there with food, clothing, books and such things, because the people there were in great trouble from a war. Mr. King was asked to go out in one of these supply-ships and live in Greece as a missionary. He was to teach schools there, and preach, and distribute Bibles, and have books and papers printed in Greek, and he was to be as far as he could the friend and helper of all the unhappy Greek people, who had been very sadly used by the cruel Turks. Mr. King said he would go gladly. Accordingly he went to the city of Athens. St. Paul once preached in Athens; it is one of the grandest old cities in the world. The people are very fond of learning, and Mr. King had a

high school there for a number of years.
He had great influence over the Greeks,
and the country will ever be freer, wiser
and happier for the life in it of this good
man.

When he went to Greece, Mr. King was
young, thirty-five years old—just at the
best and strongest part of his life. To
Greece he gave his strength, his time, his
wisdom, his love, his prayers, until he was
old and gray and ready to die. He was
not without enemies; the Turks and many
of the Greeks who are not Christians and
hate religion were angry with him. They
accused him in the papers of trying to make
trouble in the country. A man once attacked him on the public street of Athens
and tried to kill him, but a soldier was in
sight, who ran up, saved his life and carried
off the man to prison. His enemies had
Mr. King arrested and tried in the courts
on the charge of trying to disturb the
country and teach evil doctrines, but when
they came to court they could prove nothing but that he was a noble friend of the
country, a wise teacher, kind to the poor,

and setting an example of a quiet Christian life. For all this there was much hard feeling toward him. When he was to be tried before the court at Syra the foes of the gospel said they would get their way at last and he should be put in prison at Syra; that would stop his preaching for a while. Some friends went to Mr. King's wife and told her that they thought if he went to Syra the people would rise up and stone him and try to kill him. You know how Paul the apostle was stoned by his enemies. But God took care of Paul, and so he took care of his servant Jonas King. Mr. King told his wife not to be afraid; the hand of the Lord would be with him to protect him, and give him a victory over his enemies. And so it was. You know the Lord cares " for those who trust in him before the sons of men." As the hymn says,

"He makes their cause his care."

Mr. King lived to see the hatred toward him die out like a fire that has no fuel in it. He lived to see many of the Greek people regarding him as their best friend and

helper, and many young men whom he
had taught growing up to take his place as
preachers and teachers of the Greek nation.
He wrote a number of books for the Greeks,
and his fame as a scholar and as a Christian
minister was great. I don't suppose that
Mr. Maynard thought that cold winter
morning, when the boy came to him at
Plainfield school, what a learned and good
man he would grow up to be. If a boy
with so little help, no money and few friends
could succeed in obtaining an education and
reaching a place of such usefulness in the
world, I don't think any boy or girl need
give up in despair. You cannot become
wise, great or good just by wishing. You
must wish so hard that it sets you to working. Ask God's blessing and do your best.
As the Bible says, "Commit thy way unto
the Lord, and verily he shall bring it to
pass."

Now, here I end the last story of another
volume of "True Stories." I know you
little people like true stories better than
" make-up." "Make-ups" are all very

well, but when you want really to learn something you ask for a true story, don't you? I hope you have liked the stories I have told you, and that they will do you a great deal of good.

THE END.

www.ingramcontent.com/pod-product-compliance
Lightning Source LLC
Chambersburg PA
CBHW060612030726
47498CB00005B/1645